Dust, Dags, Drongos and Flies

I0593315

Bush yarns from

the outback

2nd Edition

LAURIE DICKER

Dicker Books

Web site: www.dickerbooks.com.au

Email: lauriedicker@westnet.com.au

Copyright © Laurie Dicker 2022

ISBN: 978-0-6484128-3-0

This book is a work of fiction. All names, characters, places and incidents are a product of the author's imagination and any resemblance to any person, living or dead, or to any particular organisation or place, is entirely coincidental.

National Library of Australia

Legal deposit entry

Dicker, Laurie

Dust, Dags, Drongos and Flies: Bush Yarns from The Outback. Australian humour

Editor: Rosemary Allan

NATIONAL LIBRARY OF AUSTRALIA

A catalogue record for this book is available from the National Library of Australia

To

Marjie

Judy, Rohan,

Lucy and Charlie

Laurie Dicker

Laurie Dicker was born in a small country town, lived in a number of others and was educated at an agricultural boarding school with students coming from across the farming community. Throughout his working life as a teacher, Inspector of Schools, Director of HR and Industrial Relations and management consultant, he visited numerous country centres where he took the opportunity to meet with and listen to the local characters and story tellers talking about their history, hardships, achievements and the mischief they got up to. Caravanning over many years took him and his wife to most regions in Australia.

All those experiences helped to crystallise a deep respect for country folk, an admiration for the way they forged a living against the odds and a passion for the Aussie bush characters; those open, uninhibited, unsophisticated, undisciplined larrikins with their distinctive wit and humour as sharp as a whip crack.

Laurie has published other books in the fields of education and management, a life story and his very popular Detective Harry Taylor crime fiction series.

Contents

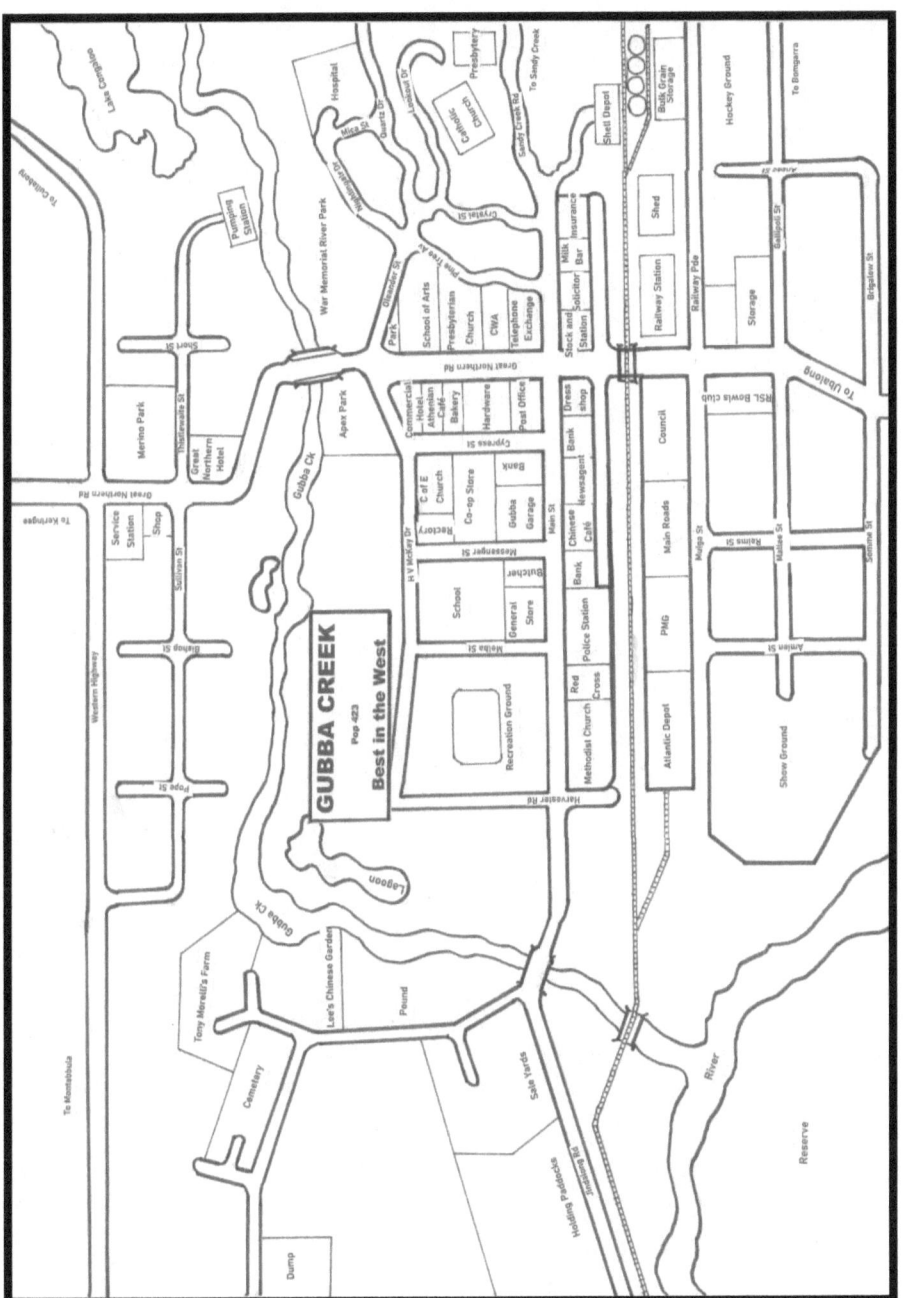

GUBBA CREEK
Pop 423

Best in the West

Introduction

While compiling this anthology of bush yarns I remembered that, when I was a young boy, my father gave me the nickname of *Speewah*. I always felt that the term *Speewah* had some mystical quality but never knew its true meaning at that time. Recently, I found that the term referred to a teller of tall tales; someone who passes on by word of mouth the unwritten tales of the outback, with each telling becoming more exaggerated for effect.

The storyteller enhanced their reputation or masculinity by bragging about the difficulties they had overcome and the hardships and dangers they faced. The telling of those tales was a means of promoting their bush skills and their manliness in a manner that appeared to be serious, but at the same time was light hearted, humorous, off handed, and matter of fact. It was the language of the outback held together by a cheeky smile, a puff on the thin roll-your-own cigarette, and a rivulet of dusty sweat dripping from the stubbled chin.

Speewah also refers to an imaginary place that is well beyond wherever you are at the moment; beyond the black stump, over the horizon. It comes from the stories handed down from camp fire to camp fire. *Speewah* is that vast open space beyond the sunset, where the dust storms are so thick you can climb up the sides and the rabbits can dig burrows into the base.

The boundary riders keep going one way because they can never find their way back. The kangaroos are so big they'll kick your dunny down while you sit on the can trying to read the fading names from the used telephone directory hanging from the nail on the wall. It's so hot in the outback that your pee evaporates before it hits the ground.

You'll know the drought is over when you can afford to put a drop of water in your mug with the tea leaves, and another drop to boil the spuds. It is so dry that the cows only produce powdered milk, and so hot that the emu eggs are hard boiled before they hit the dirt. Trees grow upside down to protect their leaves and seeds. The sheep grow cotton because it's cooler. The jackaroo sent out to check the squeaky gears on the windmills always takes a swag, some rabbit traps and tucker, because he won't get back for months.

Speewah is the land of the mythical well-known character Crooked Mick. Over the years many a tale has been passed down from one swagman to another about Mick and his exploits. He was bigger, rougher and tougher than any man around. He would eat a whole sheep for lunch followed by two apple pies and a dozen bottles of beer to wash it down. He slept outside because he couldn't get through the door or fit into a bed. He would brand the steers by biting their rumps. He would stop a charging mallee bull stone dead with one punch between its eyes, then skewer it with an iron bark log and barbeque it the next day for dinner.

As the famous Australian author, Bill Wannan once said; "If ever you come across anyone who claims to have spent time on the *Speewah* or met Crooked Mick, listen to them with deep respect, for they will be a prodigious liar."

Everyone who has lived in the outback, in small country towns or in the surrounding districts and farms, will have embedded into their DNA a little of the spirit of the *Speewah,* and a touch of the character of Crooked Mick. Or they'll know someone who fits that image. Any visitor to the outback will immediately feel that they have stepped into another world, radically different from the big city.

There's no shortage of characters in the outback towns, in the pubs, on the properties or in the bush who will bash your ear until the rabbits stop breeding. There will be wild stories of the local giants who made that place what it is today, against the toughest odds. Their spirits live on in the tales about them, embedded in the iron bark fence posts and the rusted corrugated iron sheds.

In the spirit of *Speewah,* I have compiled this anthology of yarns. I have created a fictional place called Gubba Creek with its surrounding countryside. All of the stories are fictional and all names, characters, places and incidents are a product of my imagination and any resemblance to any person, living or dead, or to any particular organisation or place, is entirely coincidental.

For those of you who have lived in such communities, wherever that might be, the characters and incidents in these stories will trigger memories from your own background and experiences.

Having lived in a number of country towns and visited hundreds of others during my working life, and later as I wandered the countryside in the caravan, I have always been interested in that special atmosphere that is so distinctive to the outback. And I have enjoyed listening to the many characters I've met along the way.

The stories in this collection are set in the 1930s, 40s and 50s, a period when the true Aussie character and the spirit of the *Speewah* still existed in the outback. The country folk of that period, together with their parents and grandparents, were pioneers. They scratched a living from the red and black soil plains in competition with fires, famine, droughts, floods, dust storms, rip-off merchants, snakes, kangaroos, galahs, and plagues of mice, rabbits and locusts.

From those harsh conditions they scratched a bare existence from the dust or mud. They fought the banks, the coppers, the visiting shearers, the government, other football teams and even their mates if things got too boring. They had no access to electricity, running water, sealed roads or sewerage services. For many, there were no nearby medical services. The men fought in every war from the Crimea to the Pacific. The women gave birth and raised kids, miles from any medical services or shops. If the

4

difficult physical conditions didn't break them, then the industrial strikes, depressions and the vagaries of the markets severely tested their resolve. But survive they did, with a steely determination toughened by that same unforgiving environment.

It was from those tough environments that the true Aussie outback character was moulded. Country people are uninhibited, unsophisticated, somewhat undisciplined, open, honest, friendly, warm, welcoming and cooperative and it was from this background that the true spirit of mateship evolved. What you see is what you get. They will walk up, grab you by the hand, look you straight in the eye and tell it as it is. They take crazy risks and explore new horizons, paying little heed to the possible hazards involved. That's how they broke in this country and that's how they operate now.

Those people work for days on end by themselves, and exist on the smell of a dirty rag. They will always stop to help and lend a hand. They are rough and tough but with a heart of gold. They would rather have a fight than a feed. They are country people, they are people people, real people, the salt of the earth. They would give you the shirt off their back if they thought you were in need.

But despite the harshness of the environment and the hardships they endured, their wonderful Aussie humour always got them through. It was the glue that cemented communities through thick and thin. It was the real spirit of the *Speewah,* that is so distinctive to these communities.

Whenever I travel in the outback, I get out of the car, look around, and try to imagine how tough it would have been for the first settlers to carve an existence from that harsh environment so far from civilisation. I'm in awe of their determined pioneering spirit and their ability, at the end of the day, against the odds to relax and spin a good yarn.

This collection of stories is a tribute to those people of the outback and their indomitable spirit and character that will live forever in the tales of the story tellers. It is my wish that a collection of stories such as this, will preserve the spirit of the outback and the importance of its influence in moulding that distinctive Australian character.

Laurie Dicker.

The Thunderbox

Ralph hated this stretch of road. It was thirty miles northwest of Gubba Creek along Cullabong Road. Especially on days like this; 120 degrees in the shade. The water boiled in the bag hanging from the bumper bar. Shade? The only shadows he could see were under a knarled yellow box tree and a small patch on the southern side of some scrubby saltbush where the sheep lay panting; heads lolling slowly in a faint sign of life. The other sheep in the distance, moved slowly towards the gate near the dry dam, appearing as a silvery, shimmering mirage above the horizon.

Willy willies swirled their dry dust dances irritatingly in their faces from under the wind-out windscreen. It was late morning and even the blow flies were unusually lethargic from heat exhaustion and dehydration. A crow sat on a dead branch, wings spread and beak open to capture any wisp of air that might give relief from the oppressive heat. Even the galahs did not take off from the table drain in their usual screeching suicidal dives in front of the passing truck.

The road was red flint hard and corrugated with gravel strewn across it. It shook every nut and bolt in the old blitz wagon that Ralph had purchased cheaply from army disposal after the war. The worn timber boards on the tray bounced up and down like the stained keys of the old upright piano in the back room of the Railway Hotel. The overworked motor blasted hot diesel fumes into the cabin, making it necessary to keep all windows open. Ralph wound out the windscreen further.

Sitting beside Ralph was Ginger Mick O'Reilly, his great mate from their days together on the North African and New Guinea campaigns. Ginger had earned a reputation as a sapper who would go behind enemy lines to lay explosive booby traps. Breakfast parades would often refer to Mick's exploits as "putting the ginger up the Nips."

After the war, they bought the blitz wagon and other war disposal machinery to set themselves up as well borers, dam builders, tree removers or any other jobs for which a farmer was willing to pay. They did the sort of jobs that nobody else wanted. They charged according to whether the farmer had the ability to pay or whether they liked or disliked that person. Only they understood their bush accounting for which there was no paperwork. They would overcharge Andrew McCormick, a rich grazier, but work for a week for Mrs Jones, a war widow with five children for nothing, providing she cooked them three good meals a day.

They lived a rough life, often sleeping under the truck, and getting something to eat wherever possible, but preferably at the local pub at night. They always carried a rifle and shotgun in the back of the truck and occasionally dined on wild duck or rabbit cooked in the camp oven after a successful shoot on a farmer's property.

The question you might ask, "Why would Ralph and Ginger need to go out of their way to travel this road, today, in this heat?"

To Ralph the reason was obvious. He wanted to see his sister Maud, who was the oldest of the seven children in their family and the one who took over the supervision of her siblings after their mother died prematurely giving birth to the eighth child. Maud therefore had a special soft spot for Ralph, the cheekiest and youngest of the brood. She was known to give a sharp backhander to anyone who picked on Ralph and few were willing to challenge her authority.

The problem for Ralph was that his sister, in a weak moment, got married to Andy McTavish; the meanest, scrawniest, skinflint of a tight arse you could find on a walk from the Cape to Adelaide. He would try to entice the local boys to ride their bikes to his farm and work for ten shillings a day to pick wool from the barbed wire fences and dead carcasses, or chip Bathurst burrs and saffron thistles with a long-handled hoe all day in the heat. They would be expected to bring their own water and sandwiches, although Maud would slip them a small parcel of goodies as they went out to work. It was not surprising that few came back.

The local farmers joked that Andy was so mean and tight fisted that he would tie a garden rake to the back of the harvester to pick up any seeds that might have fallen off the back. He was known locally as "Short 'n' Deep" or just "Shorty", meaning that his arms were too short and his pockets too deep to reach any money at the bottom when he was approached for a donation from some deserving charity in town or to help someone down on their luck. He bought second hand clothes for the oldest boy and girl and they were then passed down to the others. He took Maud to town only once every fortnight when the sheep sales were on, allowing her to buy only flour, sugar, tea and potatoes. She was expected to grow her own vegetables, make her own butter from Daisy's milk and bake her own bread.

One day, a local character, Bazza, tied a new penny to a piece of string and placed it beside Andy's truck when it was parked in Great Northern Road. He ran the string under the truck to the other side. When Andy saw the shining coin, he bent to pick it up, but Bazza pulled the string bit by bit, keeping the penny just out of Andy's reach. This farce continued until five of the local larrikins, drinking on the footpath outside the Commercial Hotel, burst out laughing at Andy's frustration. His face turned crimson, the veins on his neck stood out like creeks on a flood plain after torrential rain and he lunged at Bazza with a hatred that blinded him from seeing the small stump hidden by a clump of grass. He tripped and fell face down in the dust. Embarrassed and furious, he jumped into the truck and drove off at high speed before Maud could close her door.

For the next two months he went to the sheep sales in Bomgarra rather than go to Gubba Creek.

As Ralph and Ginger turned off the Cullabong road and drove the length of the long drive into Maud's homestead, they saw that the country was poor and that Andy had not been willing to put money into any improvements. Fences were in disrepair, gates hanging off hinges, sheds with iron missing from the roof and pastures thin and undernourished. Were it not for his sister, Ralph would have turned around, and driven back to town. Besides, she would have a big lunch spread prepared for them.

The rusty bull-nosed roof covered the wide verandah of the old weatherboard homestead with dry rot in the timber and paint peeling. At least it gave Maud some shade as she wiped her hot brow with an old towel as she waited for the boys to arrive. As they pulled up in a cloud of dust, she hugged them with love and enthusiasm

"Cripes," said Ralph with a wide grin. "Don't slobber all over me, Maud. You'll put wrinkles in me shirt. You remind me so much of Mum when she was alive. You never give a man a minute's peace, do you?"

"Someone has to look after you. You've always been pretty useless, ya know," replied Maud as she gave him a friendly punch on the arm. "And I bet you two spend more time in the pub than you do looking for some good girl to settle down with. I don't know what to do with you."

"Don't worry, Maud me darlin'," said Ralph with a cheeky smile "The good Lord will look after us. After what we've been through someone up there must be shining down on us."

"The good Lord gave up on you years ago, Ralph Sullivan. You're on your own from now on, so don't blame Him for your troubles."

Maud spent the next fifteen minutes asking ten thousand questions about their work and their love lives, and why they hadn't settled down since coming back from the war.

Maud's husband Andy came through the door and grunted; a small but painful token of recognition that his brother-in-law and friend were present. "Staying long?" he asked. "I suppose you'll be on your way soon. You'll need to get to your next job further on, won't you? There's a good hotel at Montabbula. You can stay there."

"Thought we'd stay here with you Andy for a month or two," Ralph grinned. "We could doss down in the back bedroom. Ginger and me won't be no trouble and you and us could have some of that good Scotch you've got hidden under the bed, mate."

Ginger broke in. "We heard you've got some good tin deposits at the back of your property. Thought we might put some charges into those hills behind the house; blow them up and see what comes up."

Andy quickly drew himself up to his full height, five foot eight, arms across chest, eyes bulging to bursting point, face florid, sweat streaming from every pore. "No way you're touching this property. Now say what you have to with Maud and then get on your way."

"Don't be rude, Andy. I have invited the boys for lunch, and besides, they brought us a butt of beef they picked up from the butcher this morning."

Maud smoothed down her apron and walked calmly back to the kitchen where she removed the tea towel from a fresh batch of scones.

"Now boys," said Maud in her firm, friendly but motherly manner, "Get yourself out to the toilet down the back and don't forget to wash your hands at the tank stand before you come in for lunch. It will be ready in five minutes. Don't come to the table looking like something the cat dragged in."

When Ralph returned, he took Maud aside next to the wood stove. "Cripes Maud, that dunny's bloody awful. The pit is full. You can't see where you're going through the swarm of flies and the whole thing's about to collapse. It's bloody disgraceful. Why hasn't Andy dug another pit and built you another one?"

"Andy said that one is quite okay and will last another six to twelve..."

"Bloody hell, Maud," interrupted Ginger, "that's the worst dunny I've ever come across. You and the kids shouldn't have to put up with that. The only reason it hasn't fallen down is because the white ants in the walls are holding hands for their own protection. The moment they let go to applaud a good performance in there, the whole damn thing will disintegrate into a cloud of dust. Leave it with us Maud. We'll sort it out." Ginger put his arms around Maud to reassure her that everything was under control.

Maud cooked her usual wonderful lunch. Maud's two children Spike and Lizzie sat across the table. There was roast mutton, veggies and gravy dished up on a large floral dish handed down from Ralph's grandmother. Everything was neatly arranged on a white linen table cloth covering a solid cedar table. Next to the roast was a large lemon cheese tart covered with meringue and thick fresh cream. Ralph reckoned that the lemons had been picked from the tree next to the water tank outside the kitchen. Ralph reached across the table to serve himself some roast and veggies. He felt a sharp smack on his fingers from the flat blade of Maud's knife.

Andy cleared his throat and stood to attention. "Let's say Grace. For what we are about to receive may the Lord make us truly thankful, and may He speedily help the lads on their long journey. Amen."

Having got over that small formality, Ralph; between mouthfuls, caught up on all the family news with his sister. Maud brought him up to date on what had happened during his long absences. Ginger regaled Spike and Lizzie, the two children still living at home, with

14

exaggerations of his adventures in the Middle East and New Guinea during the war. The children tried to muffle their laughter in fear of upsetting their father at the table. Andy didn't believe in small talk at the table, and was wishing the two blow-ins would soon be on their way. He was calculating how much this was costing to feed them.

"Thanks very much, Mrs Mac," said Ginger patting his well satisfied stomach and winking at the children. "That was a fantastic lunch. No wonder Andy is such a happy chappy all the time. He should be smiling all day with tucker like that? I'm so full I'll have to go down to the dunny again."

He sauntered down to the outside toilet at the back of the yard, pausing briefly at the blitz wagon to take a low powered gelignite stick and a long fuse from the box.

Five minutes later he came back through the rickety gauze door at the back of the kitchen but, before it could close behind him, there was an almighty KERRRR WOOOMPH, followed by stunned silence for two seconds, before a hail of debris cascaded in a deafening clatter on the tin roof causing everyone to cover their ears and dive under the table.

"Good Lord," shouted Andy "Is this the end of the earth? What in the name of God was that?"

They peered out through the dust-stained windows to see a screeching, swirling, darting wave of grey, pink and white as galahs and cockatoos desperately tried to avoid what might come next. The outside dunny had gone, scattered across the back yard, the corrugated roof draped over the fence around the chook pen. The chained dogs were going berserk; whining, howling, barking, leaping and straining to reach the invisible intruder.

"Shut up Bluey. Sit down Spot. Git back into your kennels," shouted Andy, increasingly agitated with the confusion. "I can't hear myself think with all that barking. Shut up you bastard dogs"

He turned towards Ginger. "What the hell did you do out there? What have ya done to the dunny?"

"It wasn't me," said Andy, trying to look innocent. "It must've been that terrible methane gas that had built up inside. I could smell it when I went in."

"Meee... bloody what? What the hell are you talkin' about?" shouted Andy; angrier with every word.

"Meee...thane gas, Andy," emphasised Ginger. "We often got it in the coal mines at the back of Newcastle before the war. If you struck a match, you'd blow up half the mine. Bloody deadly stuff it was. You could run your tractor on it. Even old Strawberry, your cow out there, gives off bags full of methane every time she farts. If you lit it, she would take off like a rocket."

Andy stared at him disbelievingly, still searching for answers.

Ginger explained. "A wisp of that gas must have licked past my ciggie butt when I threw it on the ground outside the dunny. Lucky it didn't go up while I was in there. I'd have ended up as mincemeat scattered across the top paddock for the galahs to feed on."

"Strewth Andy," said Ralph entering into the spirit of the moment, "You must have been eating a lot of that cabbage and beans lately. That's what causes a build-up of the gases in ya belly. Didn't ya know?"

"What nonsense," Andy shouted.

"Fair dinkum, Andy," assured Ginger. "The cabbage ferments in ya belly and you get bloat. When ya fart, make sure ya don't have a lit cigarette in ya hands."

Andy would have liked to argue, but did not know enough to be on sure ground. "Well, what is going to happen now? We can't go on without a dunny?" he asked.

"Leave it to us, Andy," said Ralph, squaring his shoulders and nodding to Ginger "We've got all the gear on the truck to fix it for you, Maud and the kids. We'll have a new one up in no time."

He was angry with Andy, but he could not stop smiling at the vision of white ants and compost exploding like a mini atom bomb over Andy's back yard.

For two days they worked solidly, digging a six-foot hole and then constructing a new weatherboard toilet over the hole with a

17

smooth pine seat to the right height for comfort. They then recycled the tin roof from over the chook pen fence. Andy refused to help, but counted every nail driven in as he watched from the safety of the back verandah. He often shouted questions or gave orders to show that he was still the boss of the property.

"Why are you cutting a hole in the door?" He snapped in a show of authority.

Ralph answered in a slow drawl. "When you sit here at night Andy, you can see the stars through the door; a beautiful sight, and then in the morning the sun will stream in and warm your cold bum. But most important it will let out all that excess methane gas and stop the build up after your night on the cabbage and beans."

Ralph and Ginger winked at each other and waited for a response from the skinflint brother-in-law. None was forthcoming. Andy was in the kitchen complaining to Maud about her brother and his friend and how much they were eating while they were there.

"I'm not going to feed these freeloaders for ever. They'll eat us out of house and home. Get rid of them"

"But Andy, they are building the new dunny and that will save us a lot of expense," cautioned Maud, waving a wooden spoon in his face as she brushed past him on her way to the verandah.

"I don't care. I don't trust them. What will they do next? I want them away from here. I don't want the kids to be influenced by your side of the family."

At that moment, Ginger's deep voice called out. "Hey! Andy. It's finished. Come and try out the new specialist job."

"I'm not going in there with you two. I wouldn't trust you two with a forty-foot pole"

"Okay," said Ralph. "We'll go up to the house and have a cup of tea with Maud while you try it out."

They watched from the kitchen window. Andy took his time until he was convinced that there were no hidden traps, no smell of gas or possible explosions. He would not admit it, but after a careful scrutiny he reckoned it was a top-class job and the new cypress pine seat gave it a good clean smell. He slowly lowered himself onto the seat holding onto the wall studs for security. When he was completely satisfied that it was not going to collapse, he decided to try it out.

From the kitchen window, the others could see the door was held open a little by Andy's right foot. There was no way he was going to let those meee… thay; watch-cha-me call it gases to build up while he was in there. But he kept it closed just enough to prevent the prying eyes of the rosellas in the wattle tree outside seeing the pink flesh of his thighs.

As the story of the exploding dunny was repeated with glee throughout the district, Andy and Maud's property became known as "Thunderbox Farm." They were often invited to other people's houses where they were asked to retell the saga in detail. At every house, without fail, as part of their meal, they were offered copious helpings of cabbage and beans by their thoughtful hosts.

But I have it on good authority, and I am willing to swear on the Bible as a sign of good faith, that not one morsel of any of those favourite foods ever passed the lips of one Andrew Angus Shorty McTavish again. Never again. He'd sooner starve.

Fair Deal

He was not tall; five-foot nine in his pure woollen socks. His attire was always the same, day in, day out. His Akubra hat was pulled firmly down over his right eye. His checked shirt had pockets bulging with cigarette packets, lighter, note book and pen. His wide leather belt held up his stained moleskins, tapering down to his riding boots, roughly moulded with age around his pigeon-toed feet. In the cooler weather he wore a Harris tweed jacket with leather elbow patches. When it was raining, he would pull out his trusty oil skin coat from behind his seat.

He was one of those men you could pick out easily in any crowd, and also at a distance. His silhouette was so distinctive, even in the dust and haze of a setting sun. It was his familiar stance; a permanent lean to the right as if one leg was shorter than the other, dragging his shoulder and head down that same way in sympathy.

Some would argue his lean to the right saved him energy because he didn't have to lift that hand as high to shift the cigarette permanently hanging from his bottom lip, or to tug the brim of his hat when bargaining the price of a sheep at the saleyards, or to move the flies in a slow lateral movement across his face or to lift a glass to his parched lips at the end of a dry hot day. Hat, shoulders, hips, knees and feet all leaned to the right and naturally guided the right elbow to seek out the nearest post, rail or bar for support.

The lines on his dark, tanned face told of a lifetime in the outdoors in the paddocks or at the sales yard. His eyes were steely blue; the right one always squinting against the sun, or narrowed to limit the entry of the upward drift of smoke, or flies searching for moisture. When he wanted to make a point or when he was making a deal, his eyes sharpened with a cold piercing stare. That stare held you in your tracks until he had convinced you of his point of view or locked down his bargain price.

Away from the intensity of the deal, he adopted what is referred to in the west as the horizon stance. He set his sights way into the distance. He could spot a rabbit sitting on the bank of the dam at the three-mile peg, but he would stub his toe on a tree root in front of him because he didn't see it. His mouth followed the same line as the rest of his body; exaggerated downwards to the right. His jerking forefinger often probed over the corner of his bottom lip, pulling it down and backwards searching for the gristle from last night's lamb chop still stuck between his back teeth. Those who knew him well could gauge the intensity of his bargaining by the speed by that finger jerked downwards on his bottom teeth.

Everyone knew Claude Scully. He'd been around since the year dot and had been either a bastard or benefactor to everyone in town at one time or other, and mostly both to each person at different times. One day he would be the most generous person on this earth and give you the shirt off his back, but on another, without warning, he could be the hardest bastard that ever walked, and it was hard to tell on any particular day what attitude he might take. Claude's perspective on life might have been set in concrete when he began his working life as a wool classer back in the depression when he had to work anywhere for board and lodgings and go anywhere to get a feed. He was willing to build fences, clear mallee stumps, chip Bathurst burs, pick wool from dead sheep, cut wood for the missus, sweep out the shearing shed, cut the stinking dags from the fly-blown sheep or any other task the boss might demand of him.

Those early experiences toughened him physically and mentally. He quickly learnt to hold his own in the boxing ring or behind the shed, against anyone who thought he was an easy pick because of his small stature. He rarely lost a fight. Smarter than the average shed worker, he took every opportunity to learn from his bosses.

He soon built up a reputation as the best wool and sheep classer in the country. He would stand back to look over a pen of Merinos, run his eyes over them as they moved around the yard and then move in to hold one of them. He divided the wool with his searching fingers to determine its fineness and then declare it a quality breeder. He'd mark their head with a swipe of the blue raddle. Top graziers paid him well for his decisions, because the improvements in their breeding stock from his selections made them fortunes. The sheep he considered not fit for breeding were marked with a red raddle signifying their destiny in the abattoirs.

Claude's talents became so well known that he became head sheep classer and breeder for Sir Angus McInerney, the owner of Gubba Gubba Station, one of the top merino studs in the country.

Claude raised the quality of the Gubba Gubba strain to win all the major awards in the country and made a fortune for Sir Angus. On the side, however, he was allowed to do freelance classing for other graziers and judge at major shows. He would charge little or nothing for an up-and-coming young farmer whom he respected or some poor farmer down on his luck. But there was a double or triple fee for those for whom he had little respect or those he considered cheats or layabouts or those who had made a fortune on the decisions he had made in earlier visits to their properties.

In addition to all this work he owned a small holding of his own, just out of town on which he built up a quality merino flock from young stock he selected on his rounds of other properties. Some farmers were happy to give him selected quality lambs in place of a fee; anything not to have to pay out money. But he would only select the lambs that had the very best potential for breeding.

On the way back to town along Ubalong Road, Claude decided to call in to see Jack Thomas, a farmer he had helped over the years. He had once fancied Jack's wife, Maureen. He knew there would be fresh scones or cake on the table with a cup of tea and a chance to relax away from the hustle and bustle of the sale yards with people slapping him on the back looking for some free advice. He rarely left without a sponge cake and a side of lamb as gratitude for his help.

In the early years the Thomas family had struggled and Claude had been willing to help for little or no fee. Under his guidance Jack's flock improved and the family fortunes progressed to the point where they were now comfortably well off. But as Jack's confidence and fortunes grew, he started to argue more with

Claude, was more ruthless in his bargaining on price, and was often late in paying his bills.

Jack and Maureen had one child, Tony, a boy with serious learning difficulties and a cleft palate. Tony had gone through hell at school; teased and bullied. He was variously known as Blunt, as in chisel, Candle, as in short of a wick, or Top Paddock, as in there were no kangaroos up there. He survived all that, mainly because of the positive attitude and guidance of Jack and Maureen. They involved him in every aspect of farm life and made allowances for his shortcomings.

Over the years, Jack gave him more and more responsibility. Tony, now twenty-five years of age, could do most things on the property although he was supervised by Clarrie O'Shea, an experienced farm hand who became his close friend and guide.

"G'day Mister Claude. Bit dry, eh?" called Tony as Claude's ute pulled up in a cloud of dust with the dogs barking mad, running around in circles until the door opened and they recognised Claude as a friendly face with a pat on their ears.

"Hullo Tony, great to see you again. Where're your Mum and Dad?"

"Ah, Mister Claude, they're at the top property. They took Clarrie up there with 'em to do some spraying for Patterson's Curse. They'll be there for another cuppla days."

"So, you are the big boss of the home block now, Tony. Dad must be pretty proud of you to leave you in charge of everything here. That's really good news, Tony. Good on you. I'm proud of you." Claude smiled and stretched out his hand in congratulations.

"Aw gawd struth, Mister Claude," replied Tony, kicking the dust with an awkward shuffle of his feet and an embarrassed drop of his head. "I dunno about being the boss. Dad makes all the decisions around here."

"Oh, come on Tony. I know your dad and mum want you to take over this place. You're twenty-five now and they are not getting younger. Who'll be the boss if your father fell off the horse on to his head tomorrow? Tell me that."

"Aw gee, Mister Claude. I'd have to think about that and talk to me Mum first."

"Okay Tony, I can see that you've got some lambs in the yard over there. Come with me and I'll show you how to class them. To be the big boss you've got to know how to identify the best young rams, which stock to keep as breeders, and which ones to sell. Bring the dogs with you, they can help us sort them in the yard," said Claude.

For the next hour the two of them moved through the pen. Claude asked Tony to hold each lamb while he pointed out key features such as the hold of its head, the brightness of eye, the straightness of the back, the roundness of the rump, the depth and fineness of the wool, its stamina and the way it moved around the yard.

At first, Tony was a bit shy and wanted to hold back and listen, but Claude made him take the lead and describe the condition of the lambs until he became more confident. At first, he made many mistakes, but by the end of the hour, he was more capable of seeing key features in each beast. Claude helped Tony select those to be culled for sale. He marked them with a red raddle.

Tony moved towards a young ram in the back corner of the yard. Claude got the dogs to move the mob until he could get hold of it. He asked Tony for his opinion of the ram.

"No, Mister Claude," said Tony confidently. "No bloody good, that one. He wanted to run away into the corner all the time. Don't like that one. He's for the butcher's knife for my liking. What you think, eh?"

Claude scratched his chin, pulled down his bottom lip, reached for the stubborn gristle between his back teeth, walked around the yard, caught two slow moving flies between his fingers, tugged down the brim of his hat, and leaned on the top railing while he slowly rolled another cigarette. He watched the young ram move around the pen. Tony patted the dogs waiting for an answer.

Claude had just judged that young ram as one of the best he had seen for a long time, but Tony believed it was for the butcher. The big question in Claude's mind; was it fair to take advantage of poor Tony especially when his father and mother were away at the top property? No dammit, he thought about the amount of work he'd put into helping the Thomas family over the years for little or no fee. Now that Jackie had become successful, he was getting a bit uppity, and doing his best to avoid Claude at the sales or in town.

If Claude could take this young ram, he'd add it to his own breeding stock. It'd be a first-class breeder when it matured. It likely came from one of the ewes he gave the Thomas's from Sir Angus' property two years ago to help them re-stock after the drought. He marked its head, nose and rump with two stripes of the blue raddle and one stripe of red.

"Okay Tony me boy," said Claude, "is this young ram for the butcher or will you keep it for breeding?"

"No, Mister Claude. If it was my decision, I'd send 'im to the butcher," replied Tony, with a confident swagger, and a sweep of the hand across his eyes to brush away the flies.

Claude turned and looked at the young man. "I'll tell you what I'll do for you Tony. I'll take him off your hands. I've got the in-laws coming on the train tomorrow and I want to have some good lamb for the week."

"Aw. I dunno Mister Claude. Me dad makes those decisions. I think you should wait for him to come back tomorrow or the day after. What you think, eh?" asked Tony.

"Well, you're the boss today, and you did a pretty good job classing those lambs. I think you're ready to make the big decisions now. Your dad would be proud of you."

Claude could see that Tony was embarrassed by the praise, but was still a little cautious. "How much did the lambs bring in the sale last Friday, Tony?"

"The good ones brought two quid a head," replied Tony

"I tell you what I'll do, mate. I'll give you a special deal, because I like you and you are now a top sheep man. I'll give you three quid for that reject ram, because I want some good meat for when the family comes to visit this weekend."

"Jeez, Mister Claude, I dunno. I don't wanna do the wrong thing and get into trouble with Dad."

"Your dad trusts you Tony, and I reckon he'd be pleased as Punch if you did a deal by yourself. If I could take that young ram, I could give the family a roast leg tomorrow night, lamb's fry and kidneys for breakfast the next morning, stewed chump chops for dinner, chops and cutlets the next day, followed by curried shoulder on Friday, plus brains on toast for breakfast. They'll think all their Christmases have come at once and it'd help them to remember their trip. Also, it would get the missus off my back for a week. They don't get good tucker like this in Melbourne where the family comes from. So, is it a deal, Tony?" asked Claude with a sly smirk across his face. He was happy to pay three quid for a prize young ram to add to his breeding stock.

"Aw gees, Mr Claude, you're makin' it tough on me. I dunno. I dunno if I would be doin' the right thing to let him go without me dad saying so."

Claude needed to take a decisive step quickly, so he jumped over the fence into the pen, pulled a red raddle from his pocket and swiped a stripe across the heads and rumps of two more lambs. "I'll tell you what I'll do for you, Tony. I'm willing to take that young reject ram with the two blue and one red stripe and those other two lambs off your hands for three quid each. That's nine quid the lot, and you'll be able to show Dad that you have made a good profit today. He'll be right chuffed because other farmers are only getting a miserable two quid a head. Is that a fair deal, Tony?"

"Aw, okay, Mr Claude, I suppose that's a fair deal. Do you want to take them now?"

"Good, done deal. Let's shake on that, Tony." They shook hands. "No, I've got to go down the road to do some classing for old Mr Butterworth down Barney's Lane, but I should be back in about three hours. Can you put those three sheep in the loading pen over there for when I get back, and then we'll load them in the back of my ute?" asked Claude.

"No problem, Mister Claude."

Claude helped Tony lift the three lambs over to the next pen.

As he drove away, Claude could not stop smiling, thinking of his fabulous deal; three quid for that young breeding ram. It would be a big boost to his flock and Tony would be none the wiser.

Three hours later, Claude backed his ute up to the loading ramp and started to load the lambs. "Hey Tony," he called out. "I've got the two young lambs here but where is that reject young ram?"

At that moment, Tony emerged from the shed with two flour sacks on his shoulders. He walked over to the ute, opened the side door and dumped the sacks on the front seat.

"There you are, Mister Claude. There's the young ram. I knew you were very busy this week, and you've got to meet the relatives from the train tomorrow so I thought I'd make it easy for you. While you were up at Mister Butterworth's, I killed and dressed the young ram, and I've wrapped it in the flour sacks for you. All you've got to do now is get the missus to cook him," beamed Tony, hands on hips, chest pushed forward with confidence, proud as Punch. "You gave me a good price so I thought that I'd do something in return for you because you've been so good to me. That's a fair deal eh, Mister Claude?"

Claude was speechless. Eventually, he managed a weak reply. "Yes Tony, I suppose that's a fair deal."

Law and Order

When Big Jim walked into a room his physical stature commanded immediate attention. He reminded everyone of those rough-hewn wiry timber cutters, who could eat a giant steak, six eggs and half a loaf of bread for breakfast. Never given to long speeches or lectures and never wasting energy on sudden movements unless in danger.

Big Jim was an open book to the folk in this outback community. He was Sergeant James Morris, known locally as 'Big Jim'; a tall, raw-boned giant, all muscle and sinew with a lantern jaw and short cropped straight hair. He sat on a stool in the back saloon bar at the Railway Hotel having a quiet drink with the barman, Squeaky Atkins, before going home.

Born and bred in Mt Isa, the fifth son of a Welsh miner, Jim learnt quickly how to look after himself in that tough environment; first against his elder brothers who could all go the distance in the local boxing ring, and then against the other case-hardened country kids from that outback mining town. It was a good life, but mining was not his scene and so, when he was old enough, Jim packed up and went south to the big smoke to train as a policeman.

At the academy he quickly established himself as the boxing champion, but his open, friendly nature made him one of the most popular trainees. His superiors marked him down for his first appointment straight into the city downtown squad dealing with the toughest criminals.

Following that experience he spent time on the beat in the suburbs with short-term appointments to country stations, then the armed robbery squad and later the licensing branch. He was no wowser, but Jim was never really happy with the hard drinking, hard playing and gung-ho behaviour expected from members of some of those city crime squads for whom bribery and corruption seemed to be par for the course.

So, in 1940, he enlisted in the 2/16 Battalion and saw service both in North Africa and New Guinea. His size and strength made him a certainty to be a Bren gunner and he was awarded a DSO when he single-handedly held off the advancing Japanese troops to allow his platoon to escape over a narrow wooden bridge to safety. Some say he should have been given the VC for that effort, but Jim dismissed it all as just another skirmish in the jungle.

Discharged from the army in 1946, Jim worked in odd jobs for a while, but eventually signed up for the police force again. Initially he was appointed again to the Central police squads. He gained promotion quickly, but Jim made it clear that he preferred to work in a country town. He was appointed to Gubba Creek where he now sits at eleven o'clock at night in the saloon bar of the Railway Hotel.

"Hey Squeaky," shouted Holy Moses, the local SP bookie, as he walked in the back door carrying two empty flagons. "Fill 'em up with draught beer will ya, mate? The boys are drinkin' too much at the party tonight. Have to get some refills and take 'em home or they'll all go thirsty."

He turned towards Big Jim. "G'day Sarge. Me young nephew, Tommy here, was worried when he saw your uniform through the back window. Thought we were gunna get into trouble t'nite for after-hours drinking."

Big Jim reached out to shake the boy's hand. "G'day, Tommy. Can you see my hat anywhere?"

"Yes. It's next to you over there on the bar," replied Tommy respectfully.

"Well then, Tommy my boy, that's okay, isn't it? If it's not on my head, then I'm not on duty, so you've got nothing to worry about. Pour young Tommy a beer, Squeaky," Jim demanded with a broad grin.

The four of them sat quietly discussing the local football team and their results.

During a lull in the conversation Jim got to thinking about the letter he had received from Police Command encouraging all officers to be more vigilant about illegal betting in hotels. He was looking across the bar at the short, dark, shifty character called Nick Moses. He was known everywhere as Holy Moses. He controlled the starting price betting in the town. Big Jim looked at him with a deeply embedded question mark etched into his raised eyebrow.

"Hey Holy, how long since I booked you for SP betting?"

"Ahhh..., I think that would have been...," Holy paused to clear his thinking, looked up to the smoke-stained light fittings, drew slowly on a roll-your-own cigarette, coughed and shifted from

34

one foot to the other, "…ahhh, just before last Christmas, Sarge. Yeah. I think that's right."

"Holy," said Jim firmly, "It's time for me to knock you off again. We've got to show Head Office that we've got gambling under control out here. They'll be asking questions if we don't keep some action going. Be here in the saloon bar at two o'clock next Friday afternoon. I'm going to have to book you for illegal gambling again."

"But Sarge," panicked Holy. "that'll be the third time in the last twelve months you've put the knocker on me, and the beak will fine the arse off me or put me away for a spell in gaol if I go up before him again. Can I get Rusty to stand in for me instead? He's never been booked before, and I'll pay his fine for him."

"Okay," said Jim in his slow measured style. "I'll book Rusty here at two o'clock Friday and your other mate Rowdy at the Commercial pub at three o'clock. And make certain they've got some betting slips with them. Now be off with you before I book you for drinking after hours."

As Jim wandered past Butchers Lane the next morning, he saw young Jacko Jackson and Razor Sharpe shaping up angrily to each other, determined to knock each other out. Jim grabbed each by the scruff of the neck, one in each rock-like fist and led them back to the station. He took them into the back yard and pushed them through the ropes of the old boxing ring he had set up next to the outside dunny. Once they had gloved up, Jim refereed the fight to ensure a fair contest and when things got too willing. When one boy started to get on top, Jim stepped in to call an end to that round and let them cool off a bit.

"Keep your chin tucked in, Razor. You're a sucker for a right cross. Keep your gloves up. Move around to his left," called Jim.

He turned to Andy. "You're swinging like a rusty gate, Andy. Your haymakers are kicking up a dust storm over Mrs Morris' washing next door. The only thing you're hitting are the blowflies. Now lead with your straight left. Watch his eyes and jab that thing hanging down between them."

Jim wasn't about hurting them. He wanted to channel their excess energy because they were both in the local football team that he coached, but he kept them in the ring until they were completely exhausted. Mrs Morris looked over the fence and saw what he was doing and passed some raspberry cordial and chocolate cake over to them. They took off the gloves and sat down to discuss how they could beat Sandy Creek on the weekend and how the two young lads would work together as a team.

As captain coach of the football team, Jim looked after his young players. This was especially true in last Sunday's match when Bumper Mitchell, the big prop from Cullabong, a right mongrel bastard of a man, dropped young Tommy Donoghue in a vicious head high tackle. In the next play Jim brought down Bumper in a classic tackle around the ankles. As the big fellow got up to play the ball, Jim laid his forearm across Bumper's shoulders, holding him firmly in the bent position. When the action moved away from the play-the-ball, Jim's fist moved only six inches. By the time the young referee turned in response to the roar of the crowd as the big fellow went down in a heap in the dust, Jim was already fifteen yards away in pursuit of the opposition winger. The team then lifted its performance in response to Jim's strong leadership and they beat Cullabong for the first time in four years.

By way of contrast, in the previous week's match against Keringee, Jim packed down in the scrum and found he was pushing against young Andrew McGinity, a tall, skinny kid who had all the enthusiasm of a greyhound pup and weighed in at ten stone nothing, dripping wet. Jim grabbed the kid by the shoulder, yanked his head firmly until the boy could feel the roughness of Jim's unshaven granite jaw and the boy's ear was almost in Jim's mouth.

"Listen, sonny. I'll do a deal with you. You don't push and I won't. What do you think about that?"

"Fair enough, mate. That's a deal," replied the boy nervously.

Jim found out later that the boy was home from boarding school and was filling in for the team because the local farmers were too busy harvesting to play that weekend. Jim had a fairly relaxed game that day and let his younger players do the hard work for him.

On the Monday after the Cullabong match, Jim was looking for a quiet day as he nursed the body bruises from the tough match and a thick head from the celebrations on the way home, so he was quite happy to take a relaxed stroll down the main street late in the afternoon to talk to the folks doing their shopping. But when he stopped to chat to Charlie Schultz, sitting in his truck, he saw the shotgun and six wild ducks on the front seat.

"For God's sake Charlie, you know it's out of season for ducks. Why the hell are you driving into town for everyone to see? Where did you get them?" asked Jim.

"Well, Sarge I know you're not gunna believe me, 'cause I got that feeling in me bones, but I've been doin' some fence contracting for old Cracka Wright out the back of Logan's Lagoon in that horrible swamp country. The place was crawling with snakes. And this is the bit I know you'll find difficult to believe Jim, but every time I lifted the gun, pointed it at a snake and pulled the trigger, a bloody duck flew in front of the barrel."

Charlie swung his arms in an arc to demonstrate his shooting action to Jim and how he drew a bead on the moving snakes. "So, help me God Jim, that's the truth. Cross me heart and spit, mate. Hope to die if I tell a lie, mate. Of course, I couldn't leave the ducks out there for the wild pigs to eat, so I brought 'em home, and I was just on me way to your place to give a couple to Mrs Morris to cook up for yer dinner ...,"

"Don't give me that bullshit, Charlie," interrupted Jim, stepping forward to poke a rough fore finger into his chest. "And by the way, where the bloody hell did you get to the other night when I pulled you up and told you to follow me back to the station after you had been drinking too much at the north side pub?

"Well, Sarge, you ain't gunna believe this neither. Me old truck stalled on the next corner after you took off, and by the time I got it started agin', you had disappeared down some side street and I couldn't find you, so I just drove home and went to bed. Reckoned I'd get 'round to see you the next morning," replied Charlie, lying through his teeth.

"Charlie, there you go again. The lies pour out of you like the smoke from your stinking exhaust," cautioned Jim, looking Charlie sternly in the eye. "Now you listen carefully. If I see you

38

drinking anything stronger than lemonade in the next month, I'll throw the book at you. Now get off with you before I change my mind."

"Christ Sarge, you and my Missus must've gone to the same school. You both talk the same lingo. Anyhow, Sarge, enjoy the ducks, eh," said Charlie with a wide grin. His old Bedford chugged into action leaving Jim in a cloud of black diesel smoke with three wild ducks in his hands.

Jim returned to the station office to check if there were any messages and took a call from a former colleague in the city. He drove immediately to the Great Northern Hotel to talk to Dolly Jackson, the owner of that fine establishment. "Dolly, I've just been tipped off that the Flying Squad will be coming through here on Sunday. They are dead set certain that they will scoop the pool with all three pubs illegally open on the Sabbath, like they did last year. But this time they will hit you all for six if there are any locals drinking at the bar and it won't look good for me. I don't want to see a soul anywhere near any pub in town unless they've got accommodation overnight. Do you get my drift?"

Dolly thought for a minute and then came up with her perfect plan. "Don't worry Sarge," she said. "I'll contact the others. We'll organise a cricket match at the old clay pan paddock at the Six Mile out of town along the river. The losing team can kick in with a free keg of beer for the mob. Butch can bring the sausages and Gerry the bread rolls, and we'll get some cordial for the kids. There's plenty of shade for the mums, and the kids can swim in the waterhole. Harry can drive the old school bus for those who need transport and the cricket club will supply the gear. I'll contact

Dorothy from the CWA and Maud from the Red Cross to put on a tea and cake stall and run a raffle to make a quid or two for their charities."

Jim smiled confidently knowing that Dolly would have everything under control in a very short time, but still asked, "But how will we let everyone know, Dolly?"

"Leave that to me, Big Jim," replied Dolly. "I've got the best mouthpiece in the game. Josie, my daughter, works on the local telephone exchange and anything you tell her in the morning is world news by lunchtime. I'll guarantee you the whole town and district will know by tonight and the only folk who'll still be in town on Sunday will be the dead or dying, and we might even be able to come to some arrangement about them if you want."

"Thanks Dolly. I think we can leave the sick and dying to rest in peace. I'll leave it all in your hands then. Get back to me if there are any problems."

On Sunday morning Big Jim rose early, dressed in his clean uniform and ate a good breakfast of six rashes of bacon, five sausages and four eggs before taking a quiet stroll down town to survey the scene. He saw a few older couples returning from early morning church but, on his later walks, the stray dogs were his only company.

At midday a lone car was seen driving very slowly the length of the Great Northern Road. It stopped for a while in front of the Railway Hotel and then the Commercial before driving over the bridge to circle the Great Northern.

The driver turned to his mate who was scanning the pubs looking for any sign of activity. "You know Freddy." he said. "Big

Jim has been a big surprise to me. When he worked for us in the city, I reckoned he was just a big country boofhead who couldn't organize a choko vine over an outside dunny. He was bloody useless when it came to handling the tough crims in the city. He just didn't fit in."

His mate grunted in a sign of agreement. "There was no way I thought he would do any good in this neck of the woods, especially in this mongrel red neck blot of a town. But he seems to have got it under control fairly quickly. Remember the trouble we had here last year. They bloody near ran us out of town. I reckon the bastards would have shot us if we'd stayed here any longer."

"I've got to hand it to him," said the driver shaking his head, "He's certainly cleaned this place up. What do you say, eh?"

Sitting near the door of Joe the Greek's Café, working his way slowly through a large plate of mixed grill, Big Jim smiled as he watched the lone car drive slowly out of town on its way back to the big smoke.

And by the way; just for the record, the Great Northern pub won the junior cricket match, but the Commercial thrashed them in the main game. Mrs O'Sullivan won the CWA raffle, and everyone had a rip-roaring day. They all wanted to know when the Flying Squad was coming to town again so that they could organise another picnic.

Left Hook

"Hey Mavis, throw another bucket of water in the soup, Darl', we've got another one here for dinner tonight," shouted Bazza as he bumped off the walls on both sides of the corridor, stumbling towards the kitchen; showing the effects of every drop of his over consumption at the Railway pub.

"Bloody hell, Bazza," snapped Mavis, sharp as the edge of the boning knife she held in her hand. "Don't you dare bother me now. Can't you see I'm busy? It's bloody hot over this stove, I've got to get the dinner ready, and I've got a stinkin' headache. Young Mary's been sick in the backyard, the blowflies are driving me crazy and then you come in here with a belly full of grog and want to make stupid jokes."

She walked quickly towards him brandishing the knife. "Now get out of my kitchen before I cut out your testimonials and put this red-hot poker where the sun don't shine. Don't come back until I call you. Do I make myself perfectly clear?"

"But Mavis, Mavis, Mavis, me darlin', sweetheart, jus' listen for a moment. Dinky di, I'm not joking. I really have brought this bloke home to dinner. You'll really like 'im. He's a dinkum great bloke, an Aussie champion. Fair dinkum. Cross me heart and spit. I wouldn't lie to you luv, never."

Without turning away from the hot stove Mavis shot back. "I don't care if you brought home the bloody King of England, and if ya did bring him, then you and the King can piss off out of my kitchen until I call you. That is, of course, if the bloody King is willing to get his hands dirty and go and cut some wood for the stove. Young Rusty will help 'im bring it in, if he's not too bloody proud to do that, 'cause you're not capable of doin' it."

Mavis heard a deep voice behind her. "Hello, Mrs Steele. I really must apologise for being such a nuisance," said the stranger. "I tried to tell Bazza it would be rude of me to turn up for dinner without you knowing, but he insisted that it would be okay. Now if you show me the way to the wood heap, I'll get some for the stove and young Rusty here can give me a hand."

Mavis was speechless. Standing in her steamy untidy kitchen she looked up at a finely tuned athletic figure giving quiet assurance that everything was under control. He was nothing like the usual dags, deros and drongos that Bazza dragged home from the pub without so much as a by-your-leave. The man beside her moved with the grace, confidence and poise of a real champion and with a healthy attitude to match as he came forward to shake her hand and introduce himself.

"My name's Jack Hassan, Mrs Steele, and I came to town with Jimmy Sharman's Boxing Tent for the Show tomorrow. Bazza met me down town at the hotel and invited me here for some home cooking. He told me that you were the very best cook in the land, bar none"

43

Young Rusty came through the back door. His mouth fell to the floor, gobsmacked, speechless. His mind was swirling like a summer dust storm. Was this really Jack Hassan? Was this the real Australian boxing champion, the man who beat Archie Kemp, the very best Aussie boxer? Here in our house, here right now? Wait till I tell me mates. They won't believe it. Wow. Rusty couldn't believe it. His Dad had often let him stay up on Monday nights to listen to Jack Hassan's fights on the radio. He remembered how disappointed he was when Jack gave up championship boxing after Archie Kemp died in the ring from that knockout punch.

"Come on Rusty. Let's go get some wood for your Mum," said the great man. "Now tell me son, do you do any boxing yourself?"

"Yeah, we do a bit down at Smithy's place. His old man has got a ring rigged up in the back yard. It's just four posts and two strands of rope but we have a lot of fun there every week. But I always get tangled up every time I try to do a left hook."

Before they picked up the axes to chop the wood, Jack took Rusty by the shoulders. "Here, let me show you. First, give him two short, sharp, straight left jabs to the point of his nose, then weave to duck his counter punch, then bring a right rip up under his rib cage. That'll bring his guard down. Then you are in perfect balance to come back over the top with a left hook. See?"

Rusty practised the moves under Jack's watchful eye.

"Keep your guard up, tuck your chin into your shoulder, move lightly on your feet; keep moving and concentrate on the whites of his eyes. Focus, focus, focus, don't leave an opening for him. Yes. Now you've got it. Good boy."

Mavis, frustrated at the lack of action from the woodheap called. "Are you two gunna get me some wood or spend your time chewin' the fat under the tree? How long are you gunna be, Mister Hassan?"

"Sorry Mrs Steel. We'll be right there and please call me Jack. I hate that 'Mister' business."

Young Rusty didn't sleep that night. He went over and over every word that Jack had spoken. He dreamt he was in the ring fighting Freddie Dawson for the world title, moving around the ring with the grace and balance of a champion; jabbing, ducking, weaving, ripping and finally the perfect left hook to finish off the champion. His mother didn't have to call him for breakfast. He was first up, washed, dressed and ready to go to the Show by the time the gates opened.

The Gubba Creek Agricultural Show was the biggest event of the year. The whole district flocked to the showground on the south side of the railway. Everyone for miles around prepared themselves for weeks beforehand for the big event. They came from everywhere, out of the hills and mulga, all spruced up and raring to go for the annual get together.

There were cakes and tarts, fruit and vegetables, cattle and sheep, pigs and poultry, tractors and trucks, big hats and bonnets, new dresses and hairdos, kids and pets, cowboy boots and swaggers, mums and dads, dust and flies. Heading in early were members of the Red Cross, CWA, Church Auxiliaries and Young Farmers Clubs going to the main pavilion, past side show alley, where last minute adjustments were being made in readiness for the expected rush for food or to look at the displays.

Young Rusty was a wiry little kid, tough as a mallee stick and keen to have a go at all sports, but today he was interested in only one thing; Jimmy Sharman's Boxing Tent, located in the middle of side-show alley. He stood in front of the tent looking at the colourful paintings of past and present champions on the canvas backdrops. He could name every one of them. He wasn't moving from that spot until the first session started.

At last, at 10 o'clock, the boxers in their colourful gowns walked up the ladder and onto the board at the front of the tent. Boom, boom, boom, boom went the big bass drum. Ring-a-ding, ring-a-ding went the bell, piercing the tranquillity of the early morning activity. Everyone at the showground knew those sounds signalled the first boxing session was about to commence.

Jimmy Sharman climbed up onto the platform. "Come on, come on, roll up, roll up. Who's gunna take on one of my boys today?" he shouted, trying to get the crowd excited for the big fights. "They tell me that the Gubba Creek boys are tough and handy with their fists, and I know that their reputations are well known for miles around, so let's see how good they are. Which one of youse is willing to step into the ring with one of my boys here on the platform? Roll up, roll up, come and watch one of your boys take on one of my champions. Come on. A pound or two for a round or two, who's got the courage to have a go?"

Jimmy's fighters, in their satin gowns and gloves were lined up on the high platform.

Chippy Woods called out from the back of the crowd. "I'll take on that big bugger on the left-hand end," he shouted as he strolled over to climb up onto the platform.

"Good on ya Chippy. I reckon you'll take him easily," said Dutchy Holland at the front of the crowd. Everyone was looking around to see who would be next to have a go.

Jimmy Sharman took up the call again. "Come on, come on, roll up, roll up! Today I've got a special treat for you." He pointed down to the doorman. "Hey, Knuckles, get Jack up here."

Jack walked out from the tent and climbed onto the platform.

"Now ladies and gentlemen, here beside me is none other than Jack Hassan, Australian Lightweight Champion, and he should have been world champion."

To the wild cheers and whistles from the crowd, Jimmy raised the gloved hand of Jack, standing in his blue satin gown.

"Here he is with us today folks, the one and only Jack Hassan, the best pound for pound fighter Australia has ever seen. I'm gunna throw out a challenge to all youse boys from Gubba Creek. I'll give ten quid to anyone who is willing to get into the ring with Jack and last three rounds. You don't have to win. You just have to be on their feet at the end of three rounds with the great champion. Now who's willing to have a go?"

Everyone knew that the best boxer in town was Bluey Morrison. He was a class above everyone else and easily won the district and regional championships. "Come on Bluey. You can take him on," was the call from the crowd.

After a while, Bluey stepped up to the platform to the cheers of the locals. Then Rowdy Harris, after a few early morning slugs of rum, summoned the courage to step up to challenge the lightweight at the other end of the platform.

"Righto folks, roll up, roll up, pay your money at the door. See your champion take on Jack Hassan. Roll up, roll up." Boom, boom, boom, ding, ding, ding, boom, boom, boom, went the racket. Everyone rushed to get in first and be close to the ringside. Jack stepped down from the platform and looked for Rusty. He gave him a free ticket and got him next to the tent pole at the corner of the canvas square mat.

You would have to say that the first fight was more entertainment than skill. Chippy swung wild punches from everywhere. Even the blowflies had time to get out of the way.

Jimmy Sharman's boxer would have had plenty of time to have a cigarette before the punch came anywhere near him. But he put on a good show. He let a couple of Chippy's punches land on his chest and put on an exaggerated stagger to the cheers of the crowd.

"Get after him Chippy. Come on, you've got 'im on the ropes. Finish 'im orf!"

The second fight was a good contest and turned into three rounds of skilful boxing. The crowd went wild with every contact.

Then came the big one. Bluey was a fine athlete, good at all sports. He had great hand-eye coordination and he had been trained from a young age by Billy Smith who recognised his potential. The big question was whether he could stand up to the famous Jack Hassan. There was an air of anxious expectation. How long could he last? The opening round was more caution than aggression, jab, move, jab, duck.

Early in the second round Jack gave Bluey two quick left jabs to the nose, weaved, ripped into the rib cage and then came over the top with a classic left hook. Bluey staggered back. It happened so quickly that he didn't see it coming. Jack looked over to young Rusty and gave him a wink. Rusty was beaming with pride. For the rest of the fight Jack put on the best exhibition of skill and graceful movement ever seen in town, but Bluey was good enough to last the distance with the champion and they got a standing ovation from the appreciative crowd.

"Put your hands together for the boys, folks. That was truly a great contest and we congratulate both boxers for their efforts. With Jimmy Sharman, you'll always get the best. But before I let you go, folks I want you to meet two young blokes in the crowd."

Jimmy walked over to the corner of the ring and placed his hands on the shoulders of two of Rusty's mates; Spike Burr and Jumper Johns.

"Now, it's come to my notice that you two boys crawled under the tent flap and didn't pay to get into the fights, so I'm going to give you a choice. You'll either pay triple the price of the ticket or you'll earn your entry by going three rounds in the ring. Now what's it to be, eh?"

Jack and Rusty acted as seconds for Spike while Bluey and Chippy gloved up Jumper Johns.

"Right" shouted Jimmy, "seconds out of the ring. Ring the bell. Round one"

The next three rounds were a combination of fighting cock bantams and Kilkenny cats. They got stuck into each other right from the bell. Jimmy had to step between them a number of times in the opening round.

Jimmy Sharman's first priority was always for entertainment, not serious injury, so when things got too willing, he would step in, wipe a face, check the laces, rub the gloves on his shirt, tell the young pup to keep his guard up and then, after they had cooled it a bit, he would call time on.

You wouldn't think they were mates, the way they belted each other around the ring with first one being the ascendant and then the other. Jack, Rusty, Bluey and Chippy worked overtime between rounds to cool their boys down and gave them the necessary advice to get them through the next round. After three torrid rounds Jimmy called a halt. He brought the boys to the centre of the ring and raised the arms of both to signify a draw.

"Well folks, do you think the boys earned their entry to the tent?"

The crowd cheered wildly. They had certainly got their money's worth today. Clink...clink...clink...clink...clink, clink, clink, clink, clink. There was a hail of pennies, trizzie bits, zacs and a few deeners thrown into the ring and the two boys were down on their hands and knees picking up the coins as quickly as possible.

"Give 'em a hand, folks," called Jimmy, "They were two gutsy little fighters and I'm going to give them a free ticket into the next session. Line up out the front folks in an hour for the next great contest. Get your tickets now. Don't wait or ya might miss out."

"Come on Rusty," shouted Jumper "let's go to side show alley. We've got enough money here to pay for all of us."

"Let's go an' see the Fat Lady and the Congo Pygmy," suggested Spike.

"Bloody hell, Spike. Geez, what ya talkin' about?" complained Jumper, "Fat Lady? I can see Ol' Mary next door any day of the week. Why would I pay good money to see her here? Ol' Mary's so fat that when she goes to the dunny, she has to drop her daks outside an' back in, because she can't turn around when she gets inside. Nah, bugger that, let's go and see The Wheel of Death."

"Yeah, right on, bonzer, let's go." The three of them ran down to the end of the alley to catch the next show of the motorbikes racing around in the steel cage.

Rusty's mind was racing ten to the dozen. What a day. Jimmy Sharman's boxing tent, the Wheel of Death, Jack Hassan and the left hook. What more could he ask for? This would have to be the very best, bestest, show day ever. What ya think, eh?

First Lesson

Bomber Driscoll had the confident swagger of a stockman who spent most of his time in the saddle; broad shoulders dropping from side to side as he walked, elbows out, hands open in readiness, legs permanently bowed, boots scuffing the unfamiliar concrete of the narrow footpath in the Main Street. He took his time as he wandered along from the old butcher's shop now operating as a Chinese Café, past the paper shop, across the road in front of the solid brick edifice of the Commercial Bank and on to the weatherboard building with its big sign out front.

The sign spelled, *McIntosh. Stock and Station Agents.* On entering the office, he was met by a bear of a man with a keg like girth and a florid overheated brow. He was Hughie McIntosh, the big boss.

"I hear you're the bloke to see if I want a drovin' job around here. Is that right, mate?" asked Bomber.

"Well, that depends on what's going on at the time, and what experience you've had, mate. We don't just take anyone here. No way I'd recommend you unless you can prove to me that you're worth a go," said Hughie, surveying the new man in town with a critical eye.

"I've bin drovin' for all me life since I left school, about fifteen years ago. I'm the best anywhere around here. I done cattle and I done sheep. All across Queensland, New South Wales, Victoria and South Australia. Been everywhere, mate. Love being out there on the drive. Ya won't do better than me, mate."

"Why do you keep moving? Is it because you can't get on with the other blokes in the team?" asked Hughie with a sceptical tone to his question.

"Nah. I just like seein' different parts of the country. Mind you, I've had a few blues in me life but no more than the next man," replied Bomber. "I'm a pretty easy-goin' bloke to get along with, providin' nobody annoys me. See what I mean, eh?"

"Come over to the window," said Hughie, "Do you see that woman just coming out of the Post Office across the street? That's Maud. She runs a team of drovers. She and her husband have been drovers for years. He mysteriously disappeared recently. We don't know if he went walkabout or if she dun him in, but she's dun it by herself ever since. I believe she's looking for a replacement for Paddy O'Toole who left to go back to Queensland last week. Go and have a talk to her."

Bomber squinted and moved to peer past the inside of the Stock and Station sign stuck to the inside of the dusty glass window, and scanned the other side of Main Street. He searched along the street from the corner, across to the Post Office, Telephone Exchange and Church.

"Woman? What woman? I can't see no woman," said Bomber leaning against the glass to get a better look. "There's a little short bugger comin' out of the Post Office and walkin' to the corner, but I can't see no woman."

"That little short bugger is Maud, and I'd suggest you pay her the respect she deserves if you want a job. That's the best I can do for you my friend," concluded Hughie with a nonchalant shrug. "Take it or leave it."

Bomber walked out and sauntered across the road. He was almost run down by a car and a motorbike that escaped his attention. "Git off the road, ya silly ol' bastard."

He was not used to vehicles on the long paddock. He eventually caught up with a small weedy figure around the corner, outside the hardware shop. He tried to size up this character before he made any commitment. To say that Bomber was not impressed was an understatement.

On closer inspection he confirmed that she was a woman although she didn't look like one. It was Bomber's firm opinion that a woman's work was in the home and that only men did the droving. Second, she was only five foot nothing in her riding boots, certainly not big or strong enough to do the hard yakka necessary on a drive. Third, when he called to her several times she did not reply. She was either deaf or ignorant or she didn't want to talk. He couldn't get a word out of her edgeways. Where the hell would a man want to go with a sheila like that?

Fourth, Hughie said that she didn't drink. Where did you ever find a drover who didn't drink? It's just not on. And finally, she was as ugly as sin. She had an oversized, greasy, battered hat pulled down firmly on her head, pushing forward her big bat wing ears as if to catch any wisp of breeze out on the plains. The big brim

54

curled over a blackened, scarred face. Hughie mentioned that her former husband, who died mysteriously five years ago on a drive through South Australia had regularly tried to rearrange her face.

Bomber stepped in front of her. "I hear you're lookin' fer a drover to replace the one who walked out. Is that right, eh?" he asked after he blocked her way into the hardware shop.

"Have you got your own horse and gear?" mumbled Maud as she pushed past him without so much as a sideways glance.

"Yep. Just came off another drive from up north. I'm ready to go now."

"Be at the Two-Mile tomorra mornin' at six," was the reply from the other end of the counter.

"How do you get to the Two-Mile?" asked Bomber, looking anxiously at the back of the small figure disappearing further into the hardware shop on the way to get some supplies for the next drive. There was no reply.

Maud wasn't into wasting words explaining how to get to the Two-Mile. If he couldn't get that right she didn't want him. She had just picked up a contract to move three hundred cattle up north and already had three others on the team; Tex, Butch and Dusty. At a pinch she could get through with them. Still, it would make it easier if she had one more on the team.

Somewhat reluctantly, Bomber turned up the next morning at six o'clock on the common area at the Two-Mile along Jindalong Road. Tex, Butch and Dusty introduced themselves and told him to pitch his gear on the back of the truck and be ready to get orders from Maud when she had finished packing up the camp.

Maud sauntered across towards the men. "Right, now, Tex, you take the front lead on the fence side. Butch, you take the right flank in front on the edge of the road. Dusty and Bomber, you two bring up the rear. Now get to it. Let's get this mob on the road."

Her short bandy legs took her back to the truck and trailer with a sideways limp that showed that her hips had seen better days.

Bomber was not impressed. Never before had he taken orders from a woman and certainly not a pint-sized runt like Maud.

As they got the herd moving Bomber kept watching how Dusty handled the cattle. The more he looked at him, the less impressed he was. By comparison to good drovers Bomber had worked with over the years he was at the bottom. Dusty was too slow to react to the cattle movements, too casual for his liking. He hardly ever spoke to him along the way, and in general appeared too tired to get past his own shadow. He didn't use the dogs to advantage. He held them back from the herd.

Bomber decided to take things into his own hands. Each time he went past Dusty's horse, he gave it a slap across the rump or he darted across its path in pursuit of a stray beast, causing Dusty to stop short or turn to avoid a collision. On a few occasions he deliberately bumped into Dusty's horse. "Come on, Rusty, let's get these cattle movin', or we won't get to the next camp by nightfall."

"Take it easy, Bomber." said Dusty in his quiet husky voice. "Maud likes to keep the herd quiet and movin' together calmly, and that way, they'll be in good condition by the end of the drive. So don't rush or spook 'em. She don't like that."

"Aw come on, Dusty, what the bloody hell would she know about moving cattle? She's only a bloody woman. Watch me. I'll show you good and quick."

"If you keep this up," shouted Dusty, "Maud's not gunna be happy, and when she's not happy she's likely to teach you a lesson, mark my word."

"Ah that's all bullshit, Dusty. She couldn't teach me nothin'. I've been around too long. What the hell could she do to me? I've seen big grey mosquitoes bigger than her, and they never hurt me. So, what's you got to say about that, eh?"

Bomber slapped Dusty's horse across the rump with the end of his reins causing it to rear up sharply, nearly unseating Dusty.

Two hours down the track, Maud's truck stopped.

When the riders caught up, they dismounted and walked over to the truck for a drink and smoke. Tex remained in the saddle. Bomber again tried to assert his authority by jabbing his elbow into Dusty's rib cage and then with a swift flick of his boot, he tripped him and sent him sprawling into the long grass. Dusty rose and was rushing to give Bomber a whack when he was stopped in his tracks by a sharp, high pitched shrill from Maud from the cabin of her truck. "Hey, you two, stop where you are."

She climbed slowly down, followed by an excited blue heeler dog which shadowed her every move as she sauntered over to the boys. Her right fist hit Bomber squarely on the point of his nose and, as he staggered back, the edge of her boot caught him under the kneecap. As he crumbled forward to relieve the pain, her backhanded left hand wiped all expression from his face with an almighty smack before her right hand came over the top with a rabbit killer punch to his neck.

Bomber sprawled in the dust and Maud returned to the truck. She retrieved a bottle of beer from behind the seat, clamped the top between the few teeth remaining on the left side of her mouth, and with a deft flick of her wrist removed the cap. She spat the top into the dust in front of Bomber. She poured about a cup over Bomber's face, then handed the rest to Dusty.

"You've got ten minutes for smoko and then I want them cattle on the move again. I'm goin' ahead to set up tonight." She hopped back in the cabin and drove off.

"What the bloody hell was that?" exclaimed Bomber as he dragged himself up off the grass.

"That was Maud, mate. She's the boss around here and don't you forget it, 'cause Maud only ever gives one lesson," explained Dusty.

"And what lesson is that?"

"Ya just had the first lesson mate. And if you didn't like it, and you didn't learn real quick, then get on that bloody horse of yours and get out of here faster than a goanna up a tree, 'cause Maud don't never waste no time giving a second lesson."

He Who Must Be Obeyed

To compare Jock Armstrong to an Ironbark sleeper or a length of steel railway line would be as close to the mark as one could get. His rustic red complexion covered a tough, strong, resilient, white ant and weather proof, inflexible, unflinching, straight body. You could run him over with a steam engine and he would bounce up ready for the next hit without taking a backward step.

Jock's father had emigrated from a Scottish valley high in the Grampian Mountains above Pitlochry, where he had to hang onto a birch branch with his teeth to stop the wind blowing him away while shearing a sheep on the steep slope. When the family moved to Australia, his father worked in the mines until he had sufficient funds to purchase a small holding at the ten-mile peg on the Great Northern Road out of Gubba Creek, where he raised his son Jock and three daughters.

On the death of his father, Jock took over the running of the property and saved enough of his earnings to buy two adjacent soldier settlement blocks. Those blocks had been abandoned by the diggers after World War 1 because each block was too small to support a family in that low rainfall area. There was not enough grass there to feed a crowbar let alone a family. Jock was a shrewd businessman. He was the toughest man to deal with. It was rare for anyone to put it over him. Few men could stand the intensity of those cold, unblinking eyes as they locked in focus on your face until you gave in to their demands. Everything he did was guided by a methodical plan, and when something unexpected came along, he merely altered it to fit his idea of what was right.

Only one person could break through his cold steely exterior. She was the beautiful Margaret, the wee Scottish lass who melted his heart, and who stood by him through thick and thin to develop the property and raise a family of one son, Maxwell, and three beautiful daughters, Elizabeth, Kathleen and Eileen. Margaret was a petite, fair skinned, red-haired beauty.

She was an intelligent woman who worked like a Trojan to help Jock on the farm. She also worked tirelessly for the church and Show Society in town. She had a calm disposition which gave the appearance that she was subordinate to all around her. In fact, her soft exterior hid the real strength of her character. She allowed Jock to appear to be in command in matters of the family, but she was the one who pulled the strings behind the scene, as she did in various committees in town where her quiet reasoning often won over others in authority without any wish on her part to assume positions of power.

Jock took Max out of school at age fifteen to run the farm and look after the family while he went to war where he fought with distinction in the North African campaign as a platoon sergeant. He drilled his men until they dropped, but earned their respect because of his bravery under fire. He won a Distinguished Service Medal before being hit with shrapnel in the knee and shipped home.

Margaret was disappointed that Max could not finish his schooling and go on to achieve his ambition of becoming an agronomist, but she gave in to the demands of war.

She was however more determined that the girls got to the city to be educated at the Presbyterian Ladies College. Elizabeth, the eldest became a teacher and married a teacher. Kathleen became a microbiologist and was too involved in her research to become involved with matters of the heart. And Eileen left school to join a bank which transferred her back to the city where she met a boy who she had known from the PLC dances. He was Hamish Mulholland, the son of a chemist from the inner city, and one who had never put a foot on a farm in his whole life or travelled beyond the city.

Last week, Eileen phoned her mother to ask if it was convenient for her and Hamish to drive to Gubba Creek and stay for a few days. She made it very clear that Hamish was the man with whom she wished to spend the rest of her life, and that Hamish might ask her father for her hand in marriage.

"I don't want Dad to know yet. You know what he is like. He will say no before we leave the city. I want him to meet Hamish before we spring it on him. What do you think, Mum?" asked Eileen.

"Eileen, I'm so thrilled for you, and I'm sure that Hamish is a wonderful person and will get along with your father once they meet. Don't worry about your father, he's more bluff than rough and scruff. I'll handle him. Now get yourself here as soon as you can. I can't wait to meet you both and to give Hamish a wee touch of country hospitality. All my love darling," replied Margaret, pumped with excitement at the impending visit.

Eileen was still very anxious, knowing her father as she did, and aware that he was very angry when Elizabeth got married without asking his permission. He was kind and fair but a strict disciplinarian to all his children. Eileen was his favourite and therefore she didn't want to disappoint him. But let's face the truth; this is the man who impressed the men in his army platoon with his mental and physical toughness by slowly inserting needles under his finger nails and then challenging his men to hold their fingers in the flame of a match longer than him. Eileen shuddered to think how Hamish would feel on meeting her father or how her father might respond to Hamish.

Margaret and Max saw the brand-new Oldsmobile pull up in a cloud of dust at the front gate and rushed out to meet the young couple. Eileen bounced out, skirt and shirt tails flying as she rushed around the front of the car to greet her mother and Max. Hamish was a little more cautious as he emerged into a world quite unfamiliar to a city boy. He was overawed by this sudden burst of country friendliness. His well-groomed appearance seemed somewhat out of character in these new surroundings. There were introductions, hugs and kisses all around and much nervous chatter at first about everything in general but nothing in particular.

"Where's Dad?" asked Eileen.

"I think he's out the back at the woodheap," replied her mother, still flushed with excitement. "Let's go out there so he can meet Hamish."

"Hello Dad. It's so good to see you. I would like you to meet Hamish, my friend," said Eileen with a nervous stutter. She gave her father a peck on the cheek and a quick hug.

Jock stood upright in his blue singlet. His muscles were bulging, looking as if they had been hewn from a piece of ironbark with a razor-sharp adze. After cutting logs for the fire, his skin was shining with sweat and his eyes focussed sharply on this new intruder to his domain.

"Do ye know how to use an axe, lad?" asked Jock.

Hamish replied with some trepidation, wondering what might happen to his patent leather shoes, tailored pure wool suit and starched white shirt and tie. "I think so. I used to have a tommyhawk in the boy scouts. I'm willing to give it a try."

"Then you split those Yellow Box blocks over there for the fuel stove for Eileen's mother while I cut these pine logs for the boiler. Here; take this axe. Mind, it is sharp enough to shave with."

"I'll give you two a hand," said Max trying to ease the pressure on Hamish.

"No Max," snapped his father with a glare that could split a granite rock "I want you to take your mother and Eileen into town and pick up the mail and groceries. The lad and I will look after this. Now be off with you and stop interrupting and wasting our time."

Hamish worked awkwardly at first. He was uncoordinated and nervous, which Jock took in with quick side glances to check on his progress. Hamish's soft hands and city-soft muscles quickly felt the strain and pain. They worked in silence for the next half hour until they had finished the woodheap. A ten-year-old country lad had more skills than Hamish in matters of the woodheap, but there was no way he would give in and let his future father-in-law think that he was not worthy of his daughter. Pride and reputation were at stake here, and neither of these two mountain goats wanted to take a backward step, although the tussle was somewhat uneven.

"Right, sonny boy," said Jock, "put down the axe and let's get over here to the piggery. You can leave your suit coat and tie on the stump there, and you had best roll up those trouser bottoms because it gets a wee bit murky over here."

Jock strode to the piggery without so much as a backward glance. "You see that big boar there with his head between the two sows. We need to get him out and separate him from the others before he does too much damage."

"I'll get him," shouted Hamish with youthful enthusiasm. He leapt over the fence without looking down at the pile of mud and manure that took his feet out from under him and sent him sprawling into the massive white sow and her litter of squealing piglets.

Jock climbed the fence and soon had the boar by the leg in one quick movement. He flipped it on its back, held its tusked head firmly on the ground with his boot, bound its legs with binder twine and carried it across his chest to the next pen before releasing it to charge angrily at the wire.

"Here lad, take this squeegee. As I hose this shit across the concrete floor in the pen, I want you to push it towards that drain. We need to keep these pens clean or the beasties will get footrot. After that we will shovel it all into those concrete pits at the end of the drain. It'll make good manure for the veggie garden. Hop to it lad. We haven't got all day."

After they had finished cleaning the pens, Hamish collapsed onto an old stump to catch his breath and contemplate the kind of world he had walked into.

"Come on lad, off your bottom," urged Jock. "We've got work to do in the shed over here. We need to lift those hay bales off the truck and stack them under the roof. Get moving, there aren't many of them, laddie."

The skin on the inside of Hamish's arms was burning from scratches inflicted by the hay and his city soft hands were cut and bleeding from the binder twine around the bales.

"Mr Armstrong, could we please stop to have a drink of water, I'm very thirsty." asked Hamish.

"Sure, there's a waterbag hanging on that nail over there. Don't take too long"

"Would you have a glass I can drink from?"

"Glass! Why the bloody hell would you want a glass, lad? Drink it out of the bag man. It won't kill you. We haven't got time for fancy glasses out here. And get on with it, we've got things to do down the back. Max has taken our car into town so I want you to bring yours around here."

Hamish took his time to get the car. It gave him a brief respite from the grind of work and allowed him to survey his cuts and bruises.

"What do you think of my new car, Mr Armstrong?" asked Hamish proudly as he arrived at the shed. He got out and ran his hand proudly over the shiny bonnet. "It's a new Oldsmobile Hyrda-matic. I picked it up last week. Pretty good, eh?"

"Looks like a flaming air craft carrier. Waste of bloody good metal," replied Jock with a sneer. "That could be put to better use building tractors or something useful,"

Jock walked around the vehicle. "If you cut it down here behind the cabin and took off the back half and put a tray on it, I suppose you could use it for carting bags of wheat or bales of hay. We could put on a cage, so that I could take some sheep or chooks to the sales. Come on son, let's get going before the others come back."

Jock threw some shovels, a grease gun, some wire and pliers onto the back seat of the new car and jumped in. As they drove along the southern fence, he asked Hamish to stop next to one of the short telephone poles that ran from the main road to the homestead. To reach the insulator attached to the pole he got out, climbed onto the boot and then up onto the roof of the car, leaving dinosaur footprints on the new duco. With his pliers he reattached the wire that had broken away. He stomped back down across the bonnet.

"Right, now drive down to the left through that gate and head across that paddock to that windmill on the far side."

Hamish had some difficulty handling the steering in the dust and corrugations while trying to avoid the stumps and potholes with the soft suspension making it feel like a ship tossed in a stormy sea.

"Do you see that large cog wheel up there, lad?" asked Jock "Climb up that ladder, take this grease gun and give it some lubricant. It's run dry."

By the time he got to the top, Hamish's face was beetroot, the flies were boring into his tear ducts and ears, the dust was blowing over his face into his hair, and he was having difficulty hanging on with one arm while trying to squirt grease into the cogs with the other.

"That's good lad. Now come down and we'll drive over to the edge of that dam over there. We've got a dead sheep in the mud."

At the dam Hamish spun the car around, got out and walked onto the bank. He could see the dead beast stuck in the mud at the edge. They dug a hole away from the dam, lifted the dead carcass from the mud and carried it to the hole. The stench was so putrid that Hamish half-filled the hole with vomit before the dead animal was laid to rest on the remains of his breakfast.

At that moment the huge black cloud that had been gathering all day burst, causing a wash of rivulets and soaking them in seconds.

"Best give me the keys to your car, lad. There isn't any bitumen in this paddock. This black clay is so slippery in the wet, that only someone used to driving in it can navigate their way back through the quagmire to the homestead."

Hamish reluctantly handed over the keys to his pride and joy.

"Where the hell is the clutch, lad?" he shouted. Jock searched the floor of the vehicle for the clutch pedal.

"It's a Hydra-matic, Mr Armstrong," explained Hamish.

"I asked you for the flaming clutch, not some fancy name for an irrigation pipe. Never mind, I'll just crash through the gears and drive it that way. Step out of the way lad."

The car took off with a rush, but backwards over the bank into the dam, coming to a sudden stop in the mud.

"Mr Armstrong. Mr Armstrong. Are you okay?" pleaded Hamish as he opened the door to release Jock.

Hamish's mind was in a spin as he saw his prize possession stuck in the mud, the boot now full of water. He walked to the top of the bank of the dam but stopped. He returned to the car to fetch a small parcel from the back seat and removed its wrapping.

"May I suggest Sir, that we go and sit down under that tree and take a break until this rain eases. Let's partake of some of this fine, twelve-year-old single malt whiskey I had imported from Scotland at considerable cost. I brought it with me just for you."

Meanwhile, back at the homestead, the others had arrived back from town. Eileen was pacing up and down like a nervous kitten with all sorts of visions rushing through her mind as to what might have happened to Hamish. Perhaps he had already decided to leave town to return to the security of the big city and get away from this crazy family.

"I'm going to saddle the horse to go and look for them." she said.

"No," said Max. "You know what Dad would say if you interfered in what they are doing. Leave it to me. At least I have an excuse of checking the fences. I won't be long. You two get the lunch ready."

As Max rode across the bottom paddock he could see his father striding along like a regimental sergeant major, head back, arms stiff and smartly in tune with his steps. His chest was out, defying any opposition he might confront.

With barely a sideway glance he shouted to Max, "Get back down there to the dam, son. Be quick about it. Get that car out of the water before the oil leaks out and then pick up the lad. He's not in a good way. Get him back to the house, clean him up and have him at the dinner table by half-past-twelve. I'll be carving the meat for lunch. Hop to it son. No time for talking. There are things to be done."

At exactly 12.30, Jock stood at the head of the table in front of a fine spring roast leg of lamb with crispy roasted vegetables while the others waited anxiously around the table. Eileen and Hamish held hands nervously under the table in a timid show of affection and solidarity.

"Before I carve this meat and serve lunch, I want you to take hold of the glass of fine Scotch whiskey I have placed in front of each of you. Stand up. Raise your glasses and drink a toast to Hamish and Eileen. I have great pleasure in announcing to you that I have given my permission for their marriage."

He raised his glass as the others stood. "To Eileen and Hamish; may you have a happy life and many children. Three cheers to both of you and may your union be as strong and happy as the one your mother and I have enjoyed."

Nobody dared ask how the car ended up in the dam, and neither Jock nor Hamish offered any explanation. They had sworn a pact of secrecy over a wee dram or two of twelve-year-old MacLeay

Duff Scotch whisky, with only the spirit of the recently dear departed sheep buried under the tree near the dam, as a witness.

Truthful

Buster, or Jack, as he was known when he first came to Gubba Creek, always occupied the tall stool at the end of the bar at the Railway or Commercial pubs; the first before lunch and the other in the afternoon. He would talk to anyone and everyone who came within range. All were fair game to his constant chatter.

Referred to as 'Have-a-Chat', 'Windbag' or 'Truthful' by all who knew him, he would regale the locals and visitors to town with tales of his colourful past. Most people considered his stories a load of hot air, but they enjoyed his good nature and his willingness to spin a yarn or two or three or more. He aimed at impressing someone to the point they would shout him a beer in return for another yarn or joke. It was a rare day when he didn't score a free schooner or two in each pub.

Like an old smoke-stained painting, Truthful's profile was framed at the end of the bar with his back leaning defensively against the wall, his left elbow on the bar. His worn riding boots hooked over the bottom rung, his frayed jeans were torn at the knees and were in need of a good wash. A pocket knife and watch hung in leather pouches from his belt and his shirt pockets were bulging with tobacco pouches and glasses. He had a dark, greasy, sweat stained hat tilted back to cover his neck while the brim curled tightly over his snake sharp eyes. Bluey, his dog, sat at his feet keeping a careful eye on anyone who approached his boss.

Truthful's left hand always played nervously with a box of matches, flicking it end over end while his right index finger wiped the condensation from the side of his glass of beer. A misshapen greyhound, roll-your-own cigarette, hung permanently from the corner of his mouth, miraculously stuck there while he beat his lips non-stop to the tune of another yarn. His eyes pivoted in the deep sockets on either side of his twisted, badly scarred and broken nose, and his whole face was wrapped in a sheet of wrinkled sun-dried leather trying desperately to resemble skin.

"What's all this piss and wind ya tryin' to throw at us today, Truthful?" demanded Shooter Gunn, with a laugh, as he came to the bar to order beers for himself and Charlie.

"Ya wanna talk about wind, mate. You ain't seen nothin' like wind mate until you've been in a cyclone, mate, like me was, up in North Queensland," replied Truthful slowly scratching his left ear. "When I was cuttin' cane up in Proserpine at the back of Strathdickie, the cyclone came and blew me into the next paddock. Lucky to be alive, mate; flattened the whole crop, had to brush off the taipans, browns and red belly snakes before I could get out of the tangle of cane. Next thing, this second gust blew this sheila ten feet into the air and ripped off all her clothes before she hit the ground. I had to rush over and fall on top of 'er to save 'er any embarrassment and to hold 'er down against the next gust of wind. After it was all over, I took off me shirt to cover 'er up and took 'er

72

home. She was so happy she wanted to marry me on the spot. But I told 'er I had a missus and ten kids down south, but she did agree to stay with me in the tent until the end of the season and I left town."

"Bloody hell, Truthful, that story's a bit rich for me, I'll let that story pass to the winger," shouted Tommy, the overweight Council worker, from the other end of the bar.

"Well now that ya mention it, Tommy," Truthful took a long sip of his beer and, while he still had their attention, was off again. "Did I tell ya the time I took the final pass on the wing and scored the winning try against the Poms? I was workin' in the coal mines at Newcastle. I had just dun an eight hour shift. Had to get to the footie ground in time for the match. I didn't have time for a shower, face as black as tar. It scared the shit outa the Poms. We tackled and thumped the bejesus out of them and softened them up for the first test against the Kangaroos the next week. Scored three tries that day. After the match Dave Brown and Dally Messenger asked me to go to Sydney and then play for Australia but I told 'em I had a sick mother and brothers and sisters to look after. Even the Pommy winger wanted me to go to England and play for Hull but I told 'im it was too bloody cold there and I was no brass monkey."

Puddin' Starkey, the corpulent barman, looked up from cleaning the glasses with a tattered towel over his arm. He put in his bit. "Jeez, Truthful, it's a bit hard to get me head around all these stories you are trying to tell us."

"Now you talkin' about heads, Puddin'," said Truthful, wiping the froth from his mouth, "I'll tell you about heads. Did I tell you about the time I drove 2000 head of cattle across Northern Australia from Katherine to Rockhampton. Started okay with ten

73

stockmen. Be the time we got to Mt Isa, two had gone walkabout, and another two fell off their horses and broke their legs. I had to leave 'em behind. At Winton two more got locked up by the local cops for drunk 'n disorder and damage to the brothel. At Barcaldine two more were beaten up in a fight with the local shearers and ended up in hospital. That left Jacky and me to keep the mob going. That was okay until we got to Emerald when my horse died from snakebite. Had to walk the rest of the way to Rocky. Only lost ten head along the way. Not bad eh, Puddin'?"

Chirpy Chalker stepped forward with a grin from ear to ear, cheeky as ever, a permanent grin on his face, looking for a chance to stir the possum. "Cripes Truthful, you've had too many glasses of port. Ya need to ease up mate."

Truthful couldn't miss this opportunity. "Jeez mate, that's nuthin'. Did I tell ya of the time I drove 3000 head by meself from Katherine in the Territory to Port Moresby in New Guinea and didn't lose any along the way?"

"How the hell did ya git 'em across the water at Torres Strait?" asked Charlie.

"I didn't go that way," replied Truthful, as he walked the length of the bar under a hail of laughter, hats and any other missile the drinkers could throw at him.

"Holy shit, Truthful, that was some sort of a drive you did there. You were lucky to make it all the way"

"Naah," replied Truthful, "that wasn't a drive. You should have seen me the day I drove for Dutchy Holland and Spud Murphy when we robbed the big bank in Sydney."

The drinkers around the bar were shaking their heads in expectation of another long yarn and wondering when he would run out.

He continued. "We nicked this beautiful new black Pontiac car and I drove the getaway car while they did the robbery. When they came out, I drove like hell around the back streets of Paddo, Newtown and Redfern and then locked 'er up in an old warehouse out the back of the racecourse at Randwick. A few days later when things calmed down, I drove 'em to Melbourne to get away from the heat. A stupid cop on a bike tried to stop us in Goulburn but I lost him on the back dirt road to Crookwell when he skidded into a tree on the corner. Now that was a drive."

"Did they give you a big cut of the heist, Truthful?" asked Rusty, hoping to get the good oil on this escapade.

"Naah. The dirty rotten bastards gave me a hundred quid 'n told me to piss off or they'd shoot me on the spot and bury me under concrete. So, I took off for Lightning Ridge and got meself an opal mine. In no time I found the biggest opal ever found up there, brilliant blue and red colours, fit for a Queen, never seen nothing like it ever. I kept it in me pocket for weeks without tellin' anyone. Then one night this good-lookin' sheila invited me to her tent for some Irish stew and some slap 'n tickle. She must've slipped me a Mickey Finn, 'cause I woke up in the morning stretched out on a mullock heap on top of an ant's nest, without me trousers and no opal. I found out later that the bird 'n her boyfriend left town in a hurry in the early hours and have never been seen since. Never got another decent opal agin."

"Hey Truthful, pull the other leg mate; this one plays Dixie." shouted Percy the Parrot, the local lay about.

Truthful couldn't let this opportunity pass. "Thanks for reminding me about Dixie, mate. Did I tell you about the time I went to America and rode stunt work for John Wayne in his movies? He did the still shots and the slow walks down the street but I did all the action shots..., fast riding, stoppin' cattle stampedes, taking the falls down the rocky slopes. John was so happy with me ridin' that he gave me his favourite saddle and Ava Gardner, who fancied me a bit, took me to her place for a week. Now I'm sworn to secrecy, my lips are sealed, and I wouldn't tell any intimate secrets but I can tell you that I now know why Frank Sinatra chased her around the world."

"Hey, Truthful," shouted Fred, eyes rolling in disbelief, frustrated with so many tall tales. "You're always talking about the girls in your life. Did you ever get married?"

Truthful lit another cigarette and brushed the shower of ash and sparks from his shirtfront. "Only three times, mate. The first one was Mary, a really bonzer girl but she died givin' birth to our first kid. The second one was this fabulous sort from Spain, a good looker and red-hot lover. Flat out keepin' up with her I was. But I tell you mate; life was never dull with Juanita. But she had to go back to Spain to look after her dyin' parents. Never saw or heard from her agin'."

Truthful paused to let that image sink in before continuing.

"The third one was Veronica; too frisky and flighty for her own good. Robbed me blind she did. Took me new car and raced off with the local barman, but they got it in the end when they ran

76

off the road into the river down south, both of them drowned in me new car. It was a right off."

Freddy Saunders had just entered the bar to hear this story. "Sounds like you had a chance at last to make hay while the sun shone after you got her off your back, Truthful."

A quick sip of his beer and he was at it again. "Talkin' about makin' hay. Did I tell you about the time I trained the Sands brothers. I was workin' up Kempsey way and ran into these young blokes in the back yard boxin' ring throwing haymakers at each other like threshing machines. I recognised they had some raw talent so I took 'em in hand and taught 'em all I knew and as you now well know, the rest is history with Dave goin' on to become Australian champion and he would've been world champion if I didn't have to leave 'im to go west to see me Mum."

"Shit, Truthful, you're such a fast talker; I can't keep up with ya."

"Don't know about fast talking mate, but you wouldn't have kept up with me on the runnin' track in me young days. I was a pretty fast sprinter in me day. Won the Stawell Gift a few years ago and I started from the back mark. In the lead up races, I ran just fast enough to make the next round and got a good price on meself with the bookies for the final. I won that final fair 'n square mate, but one of the judges disqualified me for breakin'."

He winked at Puddin' to pour another pint. "I found out later the bastard had put his money on his cousin who was the favourite to win. His cousin came in second behind me but he got the gift and the money. I did me dough and had to walk to the next town to get work and earn enough to get back home."

77

"Come on Truthful, stop pulling the wool over me eyes again mate?" said Barry.

"Naah mate, I wouldn't pull the wool over anyone's eyes. Honest; dinky die; cross me heart and spit; true blue." He spat a glob of nicotine into the trough. "But talkin' about wool; did I tell you about the time I beat Jacky Howes' record for shearing sheep. I was up at Blackall in Queensland where Jacky broke the record and the locals challenged me to beat the record. I busted me guts that day 'n I beat his bloody record by ten sheep. I was so knackered I couldn't spit, mouth as dry as a dead-dingoes-dongers, mate. When I recovered and went to get me money the rotten bloody Queenslanders wouldn't pay up. There was no way anyone was allowed to beat Jacky's record. They claimed I used different blades 'n I hadn't paid me dues to the Queensland branch of the union, so I was disqualified. Had to catch a lift on a wagon to get back down south agin. Haven't been back since."

"You shootin' the breeze again, Truthful?" asked Spanner Wrench with a broad smile as he came in through the bar doors, all hot and sweaty after carting wheat all day.

"Nah, mate, just enjoyin' a quiet drop of the amber to sooth me nerves. But you talkin' about shootin' reminded me of the time I cleaned up the wild pigs and ducks at Booligal?" replied Truthful.

"Ole Harry Fletcher had a problem with pigs in the swamp and lignum at the back of his property so I went out one day 'n shot two hundred pigs. When I was finished, I went down to the swamp and bowled over ninety wild ducks in half an hour. Never missed one on the wing. Harry was so happy he killed and dressed a saltbush wether for me to take home. Me frig wasn't big enough so I had to give most of it away to me mates in town. Pretty good day's work, eh?"

Just then, Sergeant 'Big Jim' Morris walked into the back saloon bar of the pub accompanied by another man of roughly the same stature as Jim. Everyone looked up, some touched their hats in recognition, but nobody stopped drinking.

Chirpy couldn't resist the opportunity. "Relax Sarge, I've got everything under control here. I had to belt a few blokes around this morning to straight'n 'em out. You know what they're like. But it's all unky dory now."

"Thanks, Chirpy. I don't know how I'd get on in this town if I didn't have you to help me. Pour me two beers, Puddin', thanks." said Jim.

As they were having a quiet beer in the back bar, Jim's mate looked through the servery into the Public Bar and scanned the drinkers with his sharp eyes. "Hey Jim, who's that bloke sitting at the end of the bar in the other room; the bloke talking his head off. He looks familiar"

"Ah that's Truthful Smith. Don't know what his real first name is. He spends a lot of time here and at the Railway pub telling stories to anyone who can put up with him, and willing to shout him beers to keep the folks entertained. He also gets some free beers and a feed from the publicans because he keeps the customers amused. Nobody believes his stories but he spins a good yarn and he's harmless and folks around town look after him and take him meals."

"Let's go into the other bar, Jim. I'd like to meet this bloke."

They walked around and sat on two stools at the main bar. "G'day Sarge," said Truthful. "It's great to see the long arm of the law keepin' things under control. You're the best policeman this town has ever had. Fair dinkum mate, I wouldn't tell you a lie, ridgy didge. Who's your mate, Sarge? You know, he looks a bit like you, doesn't he?"

"Truthful, let me introduce you to my brother, Bob."

"G'day, Bob," said Truthful, wiping the condensation from his hands on his trousers and extending his long arm to shake hands with the visitor. "Welcome to town. If you're half as good as Sarge here, you must be good, 'cause he's the best cop I've ever met. Bar none, top bloke, an' everyone in town respects him."

"I'm very pleased to meet you, Truthful," replied Bob, looking him straight in the eye while holding his hand in a firm grip. "But I believe that the last time we met you had a different name."

Truthful twitched nervously, snatching his hand back and stammered an answer. "Must be mistaken Bob. Never forget a face, mate. It must be someone else you was thinkin' about. Nah, never met you in me life before. Guaranteed. One hundred percent, I wouldn't forget a bloke as distinguished lookin' as you"

"Truthful," interrupted Big Jim, "my brother Bob here is a Senior Detective Sergeant from the CIB and he doesn't make too many mistakes when it comes to recognising faces."

Bob stepped forward, blocking Truthful into the corner of the bar, looked him straight in the eye and said, "I don't care what you call yourself these days but I always knew you as Buster Willcox. I thought those bastards had killed you down in Melbourne, but obviously you got away and changed your name. Buster, I am arresting you for the armed robbery of the Bank of NSW in Sydney in association with Dutchy Holland and Spud

Murphy and while I've got you locked up, I'll be re-opening the case into the death of your wife and her boyfriend in the river. I was never convinced that was an accident. Let's go Buster. You're nicked for good this time. You'll have plenty of time to spin your yarns to the inmates for many years to come."

Big Jim and his brother, with Truthful in tow, left through the main swinging doors onto the street, leaving the other drinkers scratching their heads, searching for something to say.

As he was falling down the steps outside, Truthful shouted back to the bar, "Hey Puddin', will ya get someone to look after Bluey, mate?"

I'm Free

I went to school
There were too many rules
And boring as hell
So, they brought in me dad to tell
Him what a slob of a son he had
So, I fought the teachers
And I fought me mates
And when they called me dense
I jumped the fence
Hey! Hell. Now I wus free.

So, I worked the sheds
As a twelve-year-old
I got no gold
But I had some mooley
We got up to tom foolery
Til the strike of ninety-one.
When we fought the squatters
We fought the cops

Then I did a hop
Hey! Hell. Now I wus free.

I joined the Light Horse
And then of course
We fought the Boers
In a dirty war
Fierce and bloody with
No prisoners taken
No hands shaken
By the British generals
So, I skipped back home
Hey! Hell. Now I wus free.

At ANZAC Cove and Fromelles
We had a living hell
And winning was hard to tell.
We fought the Turks
We fought the Krauts
That's what it was about.
Me thanks when it came to an end
So, the army could send
 Us back home.
Hey! Hell. Now I wus free.

I got a Settler's block
With little money and little stock
And a great big debt

That couldn't be met
So, we fought the government
And we fought the banks
With not so much as a thanks
For all we'd done
So, I did a walk
Hey! Hell. Now I wus free.

We went into recession
With all its depression
The arse out of me pants
With little to no chance
Of getting a job or a feed
We were in real need
So, I fought the missus
And I fought the kids
Until they up and left
Hey! Hell. Now I wus free.

So, I humped my bluey
With my faithful dog Louie
And worked the farms
For a feed and a bed
In the shearer's shed
Or slept under the stars
With the screeching galahs
So, I fought the flies
And I fought the heat

That scorched my feet
But hey! Hell. I wus free.

Now Hitler comes along
And they tell me I belong
In the god damned army
They must be barmy
To think I'll do it again.
This time I'll use me brain
I've done with fightin'
And all that rightin'
I'll go 'n stay with Widow Nancy.
She took me fancy
Back there a way
And she wants me to stay
And hey! Hell. This time I'll be free.
I'm dun fightin'.

Stinky

"Aw gawd, Stinky. Go shake yaself. For God's sake, stop fartin'," shouted Bluey McVicar. "What the bloody hell did ya have for breakfast this morning Stinky? Have you been on the cabbage and beans agin?"

"Listen Stinky," said his mate, Timber Woods. "If you're gunna fart, go down wind. That one was so powerful even the sheep turned around and ran back down the ramp to get away from it."

Rocky Stone, their other mate, added his tuppence worth. "Hell Stinky, when ya dropped that one, Timber's dog ran away and stuck his head in the sheep dip. He reckoned the rotten sulphur smell of the dip was more bearable than that one you dropped."

"Ya rotten bastards," shouted Stinky in reply. "It wasn't me. Youse lot are always blamin' me. Git orf me back. It was Bluey's dog who farted, not me. He's always lettin' orf 'cause Bluey keeps feedin' 'im all the rotten muck that Butch throws out at the back of his shop. I bet that dog's got hydatids and it's eatin' his belly away. The poor bastard'll be dead before Christmas. Now piss orf an' let's get on with dippin' these sheep. The boss'll have our guts for garters if we don't have this bloody lot done by lunchtime."

The four young blokes, Bluey, Timber, Rocky and Stinky were a happy go lucky bunch of good mates who were starting to build up a reputation as reliable workers; willing to do any type of work, in any conditions, for a fair day's pay. Today they were working for the local stock and station agent at the sale yards, putting mobs of sheep through the trench dip after the sales yesterday.

They had pooled their money to buy an old Bedford truck which they used for carting or just getting to and from farms for work. They would cart wheat, build hay stacks, scoop out dams, work on the harvests or do painting, fencing or general rouseabout work. On some occasions they would go with Stinky's dad to bore wells.

They had been mates since school days; into every bit of mischief and tom foolery that was possible to be in. They stuck together through thick and thin like Tarzan's Grip. Some blokes found out to their disadvantage, that when they wanted to fight one of the them, they'd have to fight all four of them. That resulted in a good hiding, because all the boys were handy with their fists. It was much better to play to their larrikin nature and enjoy their good humour and friendship. It might get you into some weird situations but there was less likelihood of permanent damage.

They were the scruffiest looking lot in town, mostly unshaven, hair in a mess, clothes that looked as if they had been slept in, boots mended with pieces of rubber cut from old tyres, and trousers held up with lengths of rope. They wore no socks and the elbows were worn out of their coats that were held together with one button or a bit of binder twine. But their broad smiles, friendly nature and willingness to do hard work earned them the respect of everyone in the district and they were never out of work.

But there was one major problem. Stinky Smith had what could tactfully be described as a personal hygiene problem, a permanent case of body odour so strong it could penetrate a double brick wall. Stinky never ran over animals on the road or hit a galah or parrot in flight across the windscreen, because all the local creatures could smell him well in advance, and took off for the surrounding scrub to protect their nasal passages until he had driven past.

When Stinky played in the local football team he was put out on the wing on the downwind side, unless of course the team was losing the ball in the scrums. If that was the case, he was made hooker, because the other team would try desperately to keep back to avoid contact with him. He would duck underneath them and strike for the ball while they were trying to come up for air. However, they couldn't leave him in that position too long because his own team mates complained too much. It only worked if Rocky, Timber or Bluey went in the front row with him because they were used to his smell.

He acquired the nickname Stinky at school one day when he helped O D Cologne when the local Gubba Creek sanitary can man, cleaned up the mess when two toilet pans spilled in the playground. He was quite happy to help, and couldn't see why others ran away from the smell. To him it was just like the slops in the pig pen at home. What was all the fuss about? After that he wore the name with pride, a personal badge of honour, as he was the one everyone asked to clean up whatever mess that came along. At no stage did he ever relate the name to his own bodily presentation.

How could a young man of twenty live like this? Stinky lived with his family on a small property just out of town on Sandy Creek Road. His mother died in childbirth when Stinky was ten years old, and although his father acquired a new girlfriend, she refused to take any responsibility for the kids' upbringing. Nor did his father seem to care. When Stinky turned eleven, his dad left home to go droving, because he was never happy living in a house. He had never come to terms with the finer points of raising a family at home.

Stinky's father was happiest when he went bush for a couple of months boring wells, and he would regularly take his son out of school to help. When Rocky, Bluey and Timber went with them to help out they were surprised that both Stinky and his father would come back home with their one spare set of clothes still in their bag untouched. When Bluey asked why they hadn't changed their clothes in two months, he was told that it wasn't necessary. They hadn't torn the clothes they were standing up in. Why dirty another set when it wasn't necessary.

On those well boring trips, food was what you got from the camp ovens. One oven was used to cook the damper, the other stayed permanently on the coals containing a mixture of whatever was caught on the day; kangaroo, fish, rabbit, ducks, wild pigs, a stray sheep, lizards and the odd snake. Each day they threw in a handful of potatoes and carrots, a billy of water and some tomato sauce.

They started their meal with a pannikin of soup scooped from the top, followed by a main course made up of whatever could be found at the bottom of the camp oven, slopped onto a slab of damper. This was washed down with billy tea. Now bushmen know that you can keep a good camp oven going for up to seven days before cleaning it out and starting again, but Stinky's dad kept it going for two months. Any excess fresh meat was wrapped in some cheesecloth and hung in the tree for a few days. He would then brush off the flies and maggots before throwing it into the stew.

Stinky's sister, Dorothy, left home at fifteen. There were two good reasons for her departure. She couldn't get on with Dad's girlfriend, and she discovered sex. She raced off with some drover, and the last anyone heard, she had three children by three different fathers by the time she was nineteen. She was now somewhere in Western Australia. Stinky's mates knew what he had to put up with at home, but they stuck with him because he was their mate, and he was a good worker. Despite his upbringing, he was a great character. He was fun to be with.

But his mates decided that the time had now come to act. They had to do something to get Stinky clean and presentable. It was alright at work, but not around town. They couldn't let him go to dances dressed and smelling like that. So, after work that day, while they were having a beer, they decided to have a serious talk.

"Hey Stinky," said Timber, "we've decided to help you get cleaned up and looking more respectable. You're twenty now and you haven't had a girl yet. Oh, we know Laura Fisher fancied you, but she's as ugly as sin and as exciting as a bag full of green frogs. So, for your own good we're telling you that you have to get cleaned up. You have to get some new clothes so that we can all go out to the Saterdee night dances and the pictures together without putting off the sheilas. Do ya get what I mean?"

"What the hell are ya talkin' about," replied Stinky, swinging his arms wildly in all directions. He was angry that anyone, and especially his mates, should question his cleanliness. "There's nothin' wrong with me. I wash me hands and face in the dish on the tank stand every mornin' and I have a bath when Dad gets back from the bush."

"Maate," said Rocky. "Even the skunks won't talk to you until you clean up your act. Now we want to help…"

Stinky cut him off sharply. "You can all piss orf and leave me alone. There's no way ya gunna tell me how to look after meself. And I thought you were me mates. How wrong can a man be?"

As Stinky started to walk away, Bluey became more forceful. "Listen here Stinky. We're giving you 'til Friday next week to get cleaned up. If you haven't done it by then we will do it for you. Do ya git what I'm sayin'?"

"Ya can all take a runnin' jump at yourselves. If ya don't like me as I am, then I'll go and work by meself."

Off he went, swearing and kicking up dust with every step.

On the following Friday they all came together again at the sales yard for another day of sheep dipping. As expected, Stinky had done nothing to get himself cleaned up. In fact, it looked as if he hadn't even splashed his face and hands during the week and his tight curly hair seemed even more knotted and dirty than usual. But the others had carefully thought how they would deal with this and waited for the right time to act.

Rocky stepped forward. "Stinky, you and Timber work on the sides of the dip trench, and Bluey and I will bring 'em up the race and down the slide for you."

For the rest of the morning, they worked well together but hardly a word was spoken. Stinky was very suspicious but the others gave no hint of what was to happen next.

As the last sheep went through the dip, Timber Wood walked slowly forward and gave Stinky a nudge, tripping him full length into the deep pit filled with the sulphorus liquid dip that smelt like rotten eggs. As Stinky rose from the trough, he blew yellow bubbles into the air. Timber grabbed the long pole with a hook on the end. He placed it around the back of Stinky's neck and pushed him under again. Three times he went down. After that they let him walk out the end of the pit to join the dripping sheep.

"Ya rotten stinkin' bloody bastards, I'll git ya for this. I'll punch ya bloody lights out. All of ya. Do ya hear me?" shouted Stinky trying to get a grip in the mud so he could start the attack.

Before he could get set, his mates moved quickly, pinned him against the railings and stripped off all his clothes. They hoisted him high and carried him bodily to the front of the sale yards where they dumped him unceremoniously into a horse trough. This was a concrete horse trough, one of hundreds built in country towns across Australia by the wonderful philanthropists George and Annis Bills, because of their love of animals. It is doubtful that George and Annis had in mind that their good works would be used as a public bath house for the likes of Stinky Smith. But today, that was its main use.

Rocky and Timber held Stinky down while Bluey pulled from his bag a cake of Sunlight soap, a block of Pearson's sand soap and a stiff bristled brush.

"Now Stinky, you can wash yourself with the Sunlight soap or we'll do it with the brush and sand soap. What's it to be?"

"Get stuffed," was the reply.

Rocky grabbed his legs and started to scrub with the stiff brush and sandsoap. It hurt. There was nobody else around to hear his heart rending screams and colourful swearing.

"Okay, okay, okay. Stop it. I'll do it meself. Git out of me way."

Bluey handed him the Sunlight soap and gave clear instructions on how to use it. After they were satisfied that he had washed every part of his body he was allowed to get out of the trough. He looked like a skinned rabbit; his pink skin glowing wet in the cold air.

"Get me bloody clothes and get me somethin' to dry meself. It's bloody freezin'."

"Jeez, Stinky, look at ya old fellow between ya legs, mate," laughed Bluey. "You've got more wrinkles than inches today, mate. Ya won't get the girls excited with that thing tonight, mate."

The others joined in the joke.

Rocky chimed in. "Anyone got a pen? I'm going to write BOA on his old boy."

"Why would you do that?" asked Timber.

"Because when we go to the pub, we'll bet the bar that Stinky's got the biggest dick in town. After they put their money on the bar, we'll tell them to shake the wrinkles out and it will spell BOA CONSTRICTOR. We'll grab the money and run."

The three rolled around with roars of laughter while Stinky stood shivering in the cold air, not appreciating the humour of the situation at all.

Rocky walked over and dumped Stinky's dirty clothes in a bundle on the ground. He picked up a can of petrol and poured it over them, opened the box of Redhead matches and set it alight. Stinky rushed to get a bucket to put out the flames while the others stood back laughing. Building up a head of steam, he launched into a tirade of abuse but it was cut short when Rocky walked over to the truck and brought back a suitcase and placed it in front of him. It contained new trousers, shirts, socks and shoes, plus two boxes of Sunlight soap, a red tooth brush and a huge tube of Pepsodent toothpaste.

"There you are, matey. Get into these clothes and take the rest of the stuff home. Now hurry up. We're goin' down town for a drink."

When he was dressed, his mates took him arm in arm down the Main Street. When they reached Mick's the Barber, they suddenly turned and dragged him into the chair. They held him down while Mick gave him a haircut and a beard trim. Mick finished with a liberal spray of Bay Rum onto Stinky's neck and some Californian Poppy Brilliantine in his hair.

"Holy shit, Mick," complained Stinky. "What's that muck ya put on me? It makes me stink like a sheila."

"Don't worry Stinky. When you walk out of here the girls will rush at you like bees to a honey pot. Your mates will have to knock 'em away with sticks to protect you," replied Mick.

That little diversion was followed by a mixed grill at Joe the Greek's café before they shuffled next door to the Commercial pub for a drink. After his sixth drink, all paid for by his mates, Stinky started to feel better, though he swore that he would get his own back on them.

Bluey stepped forward and called for silence from the bar. He put his finger into his glass of beer and drew a wet cross on Stinky's forehead.

"Bless you, my son. I now christen this boy, "Sunlight" Smith. May the Lord look after this boy through thick and thin. Let's give a cheer for Sunlight."

Everyone in the bar cheered loudly and drank a toast.

"Best christenin' I've ever been to," shouted Jacky Johnson.

Rocky stepped forward. "From now on, anyone using any other name for this young lad, will face the wrath of hell and my fist in their face. From this day onwards this handsome young bugger will be known as Sunlight, after the soap that created him. Thank you, Lord for this miracle."

At first Stinky was embarrassed, but then felt overwhelmed with a glow of pride as the bar erupted in a chorus of cheers and clapping.

"Come on Sunlight, let's go home," said Timber. "We're gunna go to the dance tonight and then you can stay at my place."

Tony's Grappa

"G'day Tony," said Ken Knott, otherwise known as 'Reef', to his Italian mate, Tony. "How would ya like ta go shootin' tomorrow, mate?"

"Gooda day there, Reefo. That's a great idea," replied Tony Morelli, excited at the prospect of a day out with the boys and a break away from working in the orchard on his farm down near the dry creek bed off Cemetery Road.

"Tony, I'm gunna ask Heinz Shultz and Jock McTavish to come with us because they're both great shots and they won't bring any rifles or kids with them and Jock's got two great retriever dogs. It's a lot safer that way and we can enjoy it better by ourselves. What ya think, eh?

"Fantastic, Reefo. Where do ya wanta go for da shoot?"

"I've already okayed it with Brickie Thickett, who owns the property down the back of Charlie's Lagoon, just off Jindalong Road. He owes me one."

Tony rubbed his hands. "I'll get Maria to make some meatballs and ciabatta to take with us."

"None of that garlic shit, Tony. Just give us plain rissoles, mate."

"You bloody Aussies don't know what ya missin'. Itsa good for da love making, mate."

"Okay, Tony. But listen here. There's enough water still in the lagoon from last year's flood. When we get there, you and I will go to eastern end and Heinz and Jock'll cover the other end. Once we start 'em movin' we'll have 'em circling round between the two ends. Should get a good haul pretty quick, eh? We'll get a good feed in no time."

"Do ya want for me to pick you up, Reefo?"

"Sure thing, Tony. That'd be great. Let's git away at six in the morning. I'll tell Heinz and Jock to meet us at the lagoon at seven o'clock at the old burnt-out stump."

Reef phoned Jock and Heinz to finalise the details for the next morning. They were very happy to be invited on the shoot, and had all their gear ready and packed the night before to ensure an early start.

Now those four mates were the most unlikely lot to form a close friendship, but friends they were, and if one was having a difficult time the others would pitch in to help out. Reef Knott was a descendant of English and Irish convicts who moved to the outback seeking work after they had failed to make their fortune at a number of gold field rushes. Recently demobbed from the war, Reef got a job at the Atlantic petrol depot on the south side of town.

Heinz Shultz was a descendant of early German immigrants who came first to South Australia to escape religious persecution in their home country, and then moved further inland to establish farms in areas where land was cheaper. His family was interned during World War 1, but they were allowed to continue working during the next war as they were no longer considered a threat. Heinz's property was off the Montabbula Road.

Jock was more Scottish than peat, heather and whisky. Although his family came to Australia about 1850, Jock's Scottish brogue is still so thick it was impossible to cut through it with a butcher's knife. Only his family and close friends could fully understand everything he was saying. He came home early from the Middle East after his right leg ran into a piece of shrapnel that caused a permanent limp.

Tony Morelli's family came from an impoverished area of northern Italy in the 1890's to seek a better life, and after working at cutting sugar cane in north Queensland for many years, they finally raised enough money to buy a property on the edge of Gubba Creek where they grew fruit and vegetables. Known locally as the Aussie Wogs, Tony and his wife Maria, were well liked by everyone in town even though they were not considered to be part of the local society yet.

Reef and Jock fought against the Germans and Italians in the Middle East but neither of them thought of Heinz or Tony as the enemy. They were just good mates and had been for years. The war was never mentioned in any discussions among them. The one thing that bound those four characters was their love of shooting and fishing and being together in the bush away from the worries of everyday work and family. They liked nothing more than going out early in the morning with the retrievers and guns for a morning of duck shooting. On other days they shot kangaroos or chased wild pigs in the lignum or dry swamp country.

They always agreed on some basic rules on shooting trips. They never went out on opening day of the duck season. There were too many yobbos and show offs. Jock reckoned that on those days there were so many shooters, you risked putting your hand into the pocket of the bloke next to you; they were so close. They would never go out with shooters visiting from the big city. City blokes were show offs and unsafe. No pet dogs, women or kids were allowed on the trip; for same reason. They killed only for food or to protect crops. If they couldn't eat all the catch themselves, they gave it away to friends, neighbours or those in need.

The next morning at seven, the four of them gathered at the eastern end of the lagoon to survey the scene. They saw plenty of black ducks and woodies drifting quietly on the water, highlighted by the early morning shafts of light piercing the low patches of fog. The frost on the dry grass and leaves crackled under their boots leaving sharp impressions in the ice as they crept closer for a better look. The dogs were kept under tight command so they wouldn't disturb the wildlife.

Reef pointed towards the other end of the lagoon. "Jock, you and Heinz circle around to that end and start shooting when you get past that pointy section to the left. We'll wait until you open up. That'll get them circling around the lagoon. Tony and I will wait here until you start firing."

After two hours they returned to the trucks where they sorted their bag, a total of forty-four among them.

"Right," said Jock. "I'll get a fire going and then we can pluck and clean these wee bastards before we go home. It's been a great morning."

"Christ's sake, it's bloody cold," gasped Reef, blowing steam onto his hands and rubbing them together to generate any spark of heat as he pulled his hat hard over his ears to protect the chilblains that troubled him in the heart of winter. "I've never felt so bloody cold. This would be the thickest frost we've had fer years. It's so cold out there near the water I had trouble pullin' the trigger. After a few shots I had to rub me 'ands on the barrel ta git 'em goin'. Bloody ducks had ice on their wings. Slowed 'em down a bit, eh?"

Reef and Jock walked around stamping their feet to keep warm while plucking the ducks. Feathers flew off in the cold breeze. Heinz and Tony knelt on the ground next to the truck while they skilfully gutted and cleaned the birds, saving the giblets for soup. The dogs looked on hoping for a stray morsel.

"Ha. What's the matter with you, Reef? This is not cold," laughed Heinz. "Back in the old country this would be a bright spring day. Your trouble Reef is that you have too much goanna pee in your blood. It makes you weak. You're no good until the sun is high and the temperature gets over seventy."

"Ah to be sure," chimed in Jock "You need to be standing on the shore of a Scottish loch with the icicles blowing up your cake hole off the North Sea. When the fish jump out of the water to join you around the fire; that's when you know it's cold.

Tony chimed in. "Whena we crossed a snow field high in the Dolomites mountains back home and were up to our arses in powder snow, with an avalanche coming down at you from the top, then we knew trouble was comin' in the winter."

"Ah, come on you lot, ya tryin' ta take the mickey outa me," replied Reef. "Well, ya don't fool me. I came prepared. I brought a flask of good Aussie whisky and milk ta warm me up; nothin' better on a cold morning."

"Aussie whisky?" retorted a shocked Jock. "Do you mean that muck they sell down at the Railway pub? That's not whisky. Only a Scotsman can produce whisky. That piss you're drinking is the scrapings from the bottom of the distillery at the Commonwealth Oil Refinery. They sell it from the petrol bowser at the Atlantic depot where you work. Don't drink it, it'll rot your guts. Use it to clean your tools and garage floor or killing off an ants' nest. Here, have a sip of a good Scottish malt and taste the difference."

"Ah, you're just jealous Jock because we Aussies can now produce a whisky better than you Geordies and at half the price."

Heinz was sitting back against the wheel of the truck, relaxed after a good day's shoot. He reached into his bag and pulled out a flask from which he took a long slow sip. As the liquid went down, Heinz sat bolt upright, sucking in the cold air, tongue licking his lips, his shoulders giving a quick shudder as if someone was walking down his back.

"Now there, dat's a real drink for a cold morning. Dis ist Schnapps. Ah, it warms me down through to my toenails. Any of you game enough to try one?"

"Not on your Nellie," said Reef, stepping away to avoid any contact with the flask. "I'll stick with my good old Aussie brew. Hey

Tony, you're being very quiet over there. I suppose you're gunna tell us that you brought some of that dago juice to drink, eh?'

"Many years ago, I made meself a promise," replied Tony. "I only drink the juice that is squeezed through da skin of the fresh grape; good Italian grapes. It is the only pure drink. Cross me heart, it is blessed by God."

Tony pulled the cork from a bottle between his legs. "It's why we Italians are the best lovers; we always drink the grappa. It's nectar of the Gods, tell your mother. Do ya want a taste?"

"No bloody way" replied Heinz, "It looks like black tar."

"Is that the rubbish you Ities make by stamping on the grapes with your bare feet in the barrel?" asked Jock.

Reef looked at the bottle. "Who'd drink anything that had been squeezed through your dirty toes, Tony? All that black mud that runs downhill from the cemetery onto your place and the fungus and worms and horse shit in your boots. Ya must be joking or bloody desperate."

Heinz snorted. "I'll stick to my schnapps. I don't want any of dat Italian firewater. By da way Tony, how do you make that grappa?"

"Well, I'll tell you, so listen without all the bull shita smart comments. After we squeeza the grapes we take some of the juices. We add the left overs; the seeds, stems, skins and the rest of the juice and we put it in a barrel. We tramp it all with our bare feet to mix it proper like."

Tony got to his feet to demonstrate the stomping action. "It is called the pomace and then we let it fermenta and then we distil it into the liquor. That's what we call the grappa. All of the Italian farmers make da grappa to have at lunch time. It helps to warm you uppa on a cold day and keepa you going 'til you get home at night. It putsa hairs on your chest, fair dinkum. Beaudiful, tell ya Mum. Here Reefo have a try."

Reef took a sip, coughed, spluttered, spat and swore all in one gasp.

"Holy shit Tony, that's real gut rot, I could use it to decarb the motors down at the garage or strip the paint off the walls. It's still got the seeds, stems, skins and clods of black soil in it. That's bloody awful. How the hell can you drink that piss?"

Tony stood up. "Now listen carefully, all of youse. You should always have some fooda with the grappa. Now have a mouthful of this sausage and some of this bread I baked last night and then have another try."

Reef reluctantly ate some of Tony's home-made Italian sausage and ciabatta and then had another sip. Tony passed some food to the other two who gladly chewed into the tasty treats.

"Okay Tony, I still don't like it, but it tastes much better and it sure warms you up. Come on Jock, Heinz, have a taste of this crap."

Because the others had finished their flasks, they decided to give the grappa a try. There were snorts, grunts, grumbles and grizzles and Jock got to the stage where even he couldn't understand his own thick Scottish accent. After three glasses of the powerful brew, they started to enjoy it; even more so, because Tony had ample supplies of sausage and bread to soften the effects. He also had more bottles of his favourite grappa.

Reef rubbed his stomach and gave a loud burp. "It's still bloody wog juice, Tony," he said, "but I tell ya what; it certainly warms ya up on a cold mornin'. Okay, now that we've finished pluckin' an' cleanin' let's clean up this mess and get on back to home. Tony, pass that bottle of yours around an' we'll finish it before we go."

An hour or two later Reef pulled himself up by hanging onto a stump and doused the fire. Tony and Heinz dug a hole and buried the scraps around the site. They crawled slowly into their trucks and drove home.

Sometime later; back in the Knott household, Reef's wife, Sue, decided to phone the other wives. She called the telephone exchange.

"Hey Josie, can you connect me through to Helga Shultz please?" asked Sue.

"Hello Helga, how are you? Has Heinz got back from the shooting trip yet? I think Jock drove him home. Is he okay? Tony dropped off Reef about an hour ago."

"Ya. Jock dropped Heinz off at the gate not long ago," replied Helga. "But he is not so good. I watched him stagger from the truck towards the gate with his gun and a belt full of ducks but he missed the gate and fell over the top of the fence. When I went out to see what happened he seemed to be drunk and he was mumbling something like 'grip' or 'gripe' or 'gropa' or some word like that. I couldn't understand him so I took the gun and ducks inside. They were the most valuable things. I left Heinz on the fence until he sobers up. He didn't even feel the barbed wire sticking in his belly. With the frost hanging off his ears, that shouldn't take too long."

"Thanks Helga, I'll give Dorothy a ring."

"Hello Dorothy, is Jock back home yet?"

"Good to hear from you, Sue. Well, he is and he isn't. It's like this; Jock drove into the yard and ran headlong into the wood heap. He turned off the motor but then collapsed over the steering wheel. I rushed out thinking he had a heart attack. I realised he was drunk, so I left him there to sober up. I couldn't move him so I took his guns and ducks inside and let the dogs out of the cabin. By the time he sobers up I'll have the ducks braising for a good lunch."

"Thanks Dorothy, I'll ring Maria."

"Hello Maria. Tony dropped off Reef and went home an hour ago. Is Tony okay after the shoot this morning?"

"Sure thing, Susie. Tony had a wonderful time. He said it was one of the best days he's had out with the boys. I just put a bigga bowl of pasta in front of him and he just opened a bottle of grappa to have with his lunch. We will sit down and he'll tell me about the morning. He said the boys liked his grappa this morning and he said that he will take an extra bottle or two the next time because they loved it so much. How is Reef after his shoot?"

"Well, that's why I was ringing. When Reef came home, he was very unsteady so I told him to have a shower and get cleaned up for lunch while I sorted out the ducks. I got the chip heater going for him and helped him get out of his clothes. He's under the shower now... Hold it a minute Maria, he's calling out to me from the bathroom. I'll be back in a minute."

Sue left the phone hanging from the wall set while she rushed through the kitchen to the bathroom out the back. Maria waited patiently.

"Ah hello Maria, I'm back again. I don't know what they had this morning but Reef is kneeling in the bath on all fours screaming that the water from the shower knocked him over and was so strong that he couldn't stand up again. He was swearing he wouldn't touch the grapes again. I don't know what all that was about so I turned off the shower. When he gets cold, he might be sober enough to get out by himself. You know Maria, they are just like kids. What will we do with them? I better go and throw a towel over him or I'll never hear the end of it. See ya."

Mary

Well, to be sure, the arrival of young Mary Doyle at the local hospital was a big surprise. Her mother, at age 45, hadn't planned on another child and old Paddy, five years older, certainly didn't want an extra mouth to feed or another young brat crying at night. Was it the leprechauns playing their little tricks on them, or had they celebrated too long on the Irish whiskey nine months ago after last year's harvest?

Paddy and Molly had to accept in good grace the numerous jibes from family and friends about the carelessness of Catholics, and their helpful advice about what caused these things to happen. But one look at the beautiful Mary with her dark hair, pearly skin and cute little smile melted all of their hearts and convinced them that she was indeed a gift from heaven. Philosophically her mother believed that Mary was sent by God to replace Joseph, her eldest son, who was killed during the Japanese invasion on Singapore.

Their eldest daughter, Kathleen, was highly amused at the thought that her three young children were older than their new Aunty Mary. She jokingly offered advice to her mother on how she might raise her new daughter. Kathleen returned home whenever possible to help her mum, even though she and husband Graham had bought a property forty miles further east past Bomgarra. She also liked to visit home to be a moral support for Frank, her oldest living brother, who had been badly crippled by a bomb blast in the Middle East, and was in constant pain and no longer able to work on the farm.

Frank suffered the mental anguish of his war experiences and lived on Bex and Vincent pain powders washed down with any fluid available. Michael, the youngest son kept the farm going, since his father could no longer do the heavy work. The farm was a large mixed wheat, sheep and cattle property, five miles out of town, south of the railway crossing.

At the hospital to see the newborn Mary, were Elizabeth Franklin and her nine-year-old son Tom, great friends of the Doyles. Paddy Doyle would often drop in on the Franklins with a load of wood or a dressed lamb, especially after Tom's father Brian, his best mate, sailed for the western front. He knew that Elizabeth was doing it tough looking after three young boys and that she had taken up dress-making again to supplement her meagre payments from Brian's army pay.

Young Tom liked Paddy. He listened to his friendly advice and always enjoyed visiting his farm to help with the chores. It reminded him of the times he visited his Grandparents' soldier settlement block before the drought and repayments to the government drove them into debt.

Old Paddy taught Tom how to ride the stock horses and drive the tractor in a straight line and he often asked him to help around the property. He paid Tom a few shillings to supplement what the boy earned working on weekends in the butcher shop or at the sales yard during the holidays. Tom loved farm life and made up his mind early that he wanted to work on the land.

The sight of the new born baby captivated the young lad. He couldn't keep his eyes off Mary, she was the most beautiful thing he had ever seen and more particularly when she wrapped her tiny hand around his finger and pulled it to her mouth. It amazed and amused all of the women present to think that a nine-year-old boy would be so fascinated and so attentive with a baby girl. But Tom had two younger brothers, both ruffians and pests of the first order. He was pleased to think of this sweet innocent happy baby as a younger sister and was ecstatic when Mrs Doyle agreed to let him nurse the baby in the lounge chair in the corner of the room.

Over the next couple of years, Tom grasped every opportunity to visit the Doyle's farm and help Michael and Paddy with working the sheep and cattle, harvesting the wheat or oats, sewing wheat bags, baling hay, marking lambs or driving the second tractor when planting, harvesting or scarifying. Even milking the house cows and feeding the chooks were a pleasure to him and a welcome respite for Mrs Doyle to whom that task normally fell.

He loved farming so much that he pestered Paddy and Michael with a thousand questions every day. But the other incentive for young Tom's visits was the sheer delight at being with Mary as she grew up.

She, in turn, couldn't get enough of her "Toddy" as she called him; her face lighting up every time he walked into the room. She would crawl and wriggle towards him, hang onto his leg until he picked her up and played games or read to her.

By the time she was three, Mary was riding her own small Shetland pony, a birthday present from her father. It wasn't long before she insisted on helping Tom and Michael round up the sheep, shifting them from one paddock to another or bringing them in for shearing or crutching.

By the time she turned five, she was allowed to help them drove the cattle the five miles into town for the sales. On those trips she always rode close to Tom, asking questions about his school, his friends and anything that crossed her mind. By then Tom was fourteen and an accomplished rider. He kept his horse between Mary and the herd, protecting her from maverick steers that might break quickly and frighten her pony. He never ceased to be amazed at Mary's thirst for knowledge and how quickly she understood.

School could not come quickly enough for Mary. She soon established herself as the brightest pupil in the school and by the time she reached fourth class she was the outstanding athlete in the school, no doubt the result of her time in the saddle and the many hours playing bat and ball with Tom, who gave her little quarter in those contests.

By age ten, Mary was a tall, dark haired, intelligent and attractive young girl with a friendly personality; liked by everyone she met. She was at ease in meeting people from all walks of life and the other students looked up to her as the natural leader in their group. Tom was certain that Mary had a great future and often suggested to her parents that she should be sent to a boarding school to complete her secondary education in preparation for a university degree and employment in a profession like teaching, medicine or law.

"Go talk to Paddy about that, Tom. I agree with you, but I'm not so sure about her father," cautioned Molly Doyle.

Paddy dismissed Tom's suggestion. "I can't see any sense paying good money in educating a girl when all she'll do is go and get married like Kathleen and the other girls. Her job will be to look after her husband and raise a family. Any extra money I spend on her education will go down the drain. I'd rather put it towards a new header or tractor. That will be more productive in the long run don't you think, Tom, eh? At least I'll be able to see a return on my money that way."

Out of respect for Paddy, Tom didn't reply but he felt shattered. Mary would not be able to reach her true potential.

When Tom completed his secondary education, he was successful in winning a scholarship to the Agricultural College to take up his life's dream of becoming an agronomist. He enjoyed boarding at the college and he was only about 150 miles from home by train, making it easy for him to return for the holidays. When he was at home, he would take every opportunity to work on the Doyle's property to gain more experience and to earn money for the next term. He would ride his bike along the main road from home, cross over the railway line and then the 5 miles of dirt road to the property where he would work all day before riding home late in the afternoon.

Mary peppered Tom with questions about college life, and in particular about his friends; especially the three foreigners who came from Greece, Tonga and Canada. She wanted to know all about them; their countries, culture and language and how different they were from Australians. She looked on Tom as a big brother and

111

he, in turn, was amazed at how quickly Mary was growing up with her persistent thirst for knowledge.

When Tom worked on the farm, Mary would ride out into the paddock with their morning tea and lunch and would help them round up sheep or cattle and drive the tractor while Tom filled and sewed the bags. They worked together well as a team and took the pressure off Michael and Paddy. They enjoyed each other's company, sharing jokes, playing games and sharing personal thoughts and feelings.

Tom often thought of Mary's potential and what she might have achieved given the opportunity. She had everything; personality, looks, intelligence, energy, drive, enthusiasm, a positive attitude and she was liked by everyone she met. He wondered who might be the lucky bloke who would end up as her husband, knowing full well that, in a small town like this, he would have to be Catholic and probably a farmer.

Tom couldn't think of any kid in town that fitted the bill. As Mary matured into a young teenager, Tom realised that his feelings for Mary were changing from 'big brother' more towards being her serious friend and protector. Mary's infatuated response encouraged this attitude. It could not be called a serious romance, but feelings between the two were very strong and were certainly flirtatious and becoming more so with each visit.

Tom completed his college diploma, and at age twenty-three, returned home to do some casual work before starting work with the Agricultural Department as an agronomist. He told his mother he would ride out to the Doyles to see if Paddy had any work for him. As he peddled his bike past the railway station, he saw what appeared to be a train engine and a number of trucks stopped at the crossing half a mile down the track.

He thought it strange, because the passenger train came through to Gubba Creek only on Wednesdays and Saturdays, not on Monday. It must be a goods train, but it wasn't moving. As Tom got closer, he saw what appeared to be a heap of twisted metal in front of the train engine. There must have been a smash at the crossing. How could that happen? The road had clear vision both ways, and although there were no barriers, everyone was always careful at that junction. Whoever it was must have thought there were no trains today or they were total strangers to the town.

As he got closer, he saw that the tangled mess appeared to be an old canvas topped car with wooden spoked wheels; about a 1920's model.

"My God, it's Paddy's car," shouted Tom as he recognised the old Dodge crumpled in front of the engine. He could see Old Paddy slumped across the broken steering wheel in the front seat with men trying desperately to lever the metal away from his body. His head was covered with blood and he looked in a very bad shape. Father Murphy, the local priest, appeared to be giving Paddy the last rites without getting in the way of the rescuers.

Tom dropped his bike and ran towards the crumpled mess. But before he got there, he was stopped in his tracks by Jimmy Jackson, the railway assistant. Jimmy took him firmly by the shoulders and held him tight.

"Stay back, Tom. Let the boys do their job of getting Paddy out. Don't get in their way. He's in a bad way and they need to get him out quickly and down to the hospital. It's his only chance."

"What happened? Paddy knows this crossing like his own property. He comes across it nearly every day"

"Someone said that he was looking the other way," replied Jimmy. "He was watching Michael bringing cattle into town across the common over there. He wouldn't have expected a train today."

"Thank God there was no one in the car with him," said Tom.

"I'm sorry Tom. Mary was with him," said Jimmy.

"What? What are you talking about? Where is she? Is she okay? I want to see her. Tell me. Where is she?"

"I'm so sorry, Tom. She didn't make it. She took the full brunt of the crash. They got her out but she's on the back of Clarrie's truck over there."

Tom spun around. But Jimmy held him more tightly. On the back of Clarrie's truck, he saw an old, grey, oil-stained tarpaulin forming a shapeless heap on the tray held down by two drums. Mary was under that tarp.

Tom wanted desperately to see for himself; he needed proof. He wanted to lift that tarp and hold Mary in his arms and tell her how sorry he was that he had slept in that morning. Had he been at the farm earlier he might have been in the car with Paddy instead of Mary. Had he been at the farm they might have been delayed, talking, and this terrible accident would not have happened.

"For Christ's sake Jimmy, let me go," demanded Tom.

"No Tom. Let it be. Remember her as she was. You wouldn't want to see her now. Let her rest in peace," said Jimmy.

Father Murphy approached from the crash site. "Listen to Jimmy, Tom. Remember Mary as she was and how she has always been in your heart. She's in God's care now."

"But how could this happen, Father? How could this happen to such a beautiful girl as Mary? Why Father? Why?" screamed Tom, tears pouring down his face.

"It's God's will, Tom. It's not for us to question why," said Father Murphy trying to hold his own emotions in check.

"That's bullshit, Father and you know it," shouted Tom throwing his hands in the air in desperation.

"Tom, what the Lord giveth, the Lord taketh away. Search deep into your heart Tom. Find God and He will provide the answers," pleaded Father Murphy.

"Father, why the bloody hell didn't God take me instead? I've done things I'm not proud of. Why not me, Father? Why Mary?"

"Take it easy, Tom," cautioned Jimmy. "It's not Father Murphy's fault. He is suffering like all of us. Let him go. He's got enough on his hands as it is. Let it go. Off you go Father. I'll take care of this."

Tom broke away from Jimmy's grasp, ran to his bike and peddled as fast as he could down the dirt road towards the Doyles. But after a couple of miles, he collapsed in a lather of sweat and emotional exhaustion at the old yellow box tree at the bend in the road. As he fell against the rough bark, tears streamed down his face.

"Where are you, God?" he pleaded. "Please tell me why you did this to Mary. Why the bloody hell did you take Mary? Why

Mary, for Christ's sake. Couldn't you have picked on somebody else? Why should I even believe in you anymore?"

He fell silent. Nothing could be heard but his heavy breathing. The atmosphere around him was deathly quiet. Not a leaf moved in the still dry air. There was no sound of birds. Even the flies stopped competing for the drops of moisture on his face. The pulse in his temples sounded like drum beats.

"Why God? Why?" he whispered

After a while Tom picked up his bike and walked back to town, kicking up dust to both sides of the track, picking an odd leaf from a branch, breaking a twig, and watching the odd butterfly dance across the grass in front of him.

O D Cologne

He was christened Oscar Dieter Kuhn, but when his parents immigrated to Australia to escape religious persecution in their home country, they anglicised their surname to Collins. After arriving in Adelaide, they moved to Melbourne and then to Albury in the Riverina where they established themselves as mixed farmers. During the depression when there was pressure on the family income, Oscar left home and drifted around the countryside looking for work.

He was a tall, strong, muscular, sinewy, thirty-year-old, willing to take on any work for food and a place to put down his swag. His blond hair, blue eyes, good looks and personal charm certainly helped to get him many jobs, especially if the first person he met on the property was the farmer's wife, delighted to have such a personable young man to help cut wood and do other chores around the house. It was also more exciting to have someone who could talk intelligently on world affairs over a cup of tea and who had some grace and good manners.

Most of the men on the properties and in the town were initially suspicious of Oscar's Germanic background. Many of them had recently returned from the Great War and there were a few occasions when he had to fight his way to a standstill before he could sit down and explain his family's reasons for leaving their home country.

After a few beers he generally won them over and they developed a healthy respect for his physical prowess and willingness to do a hard day's work. He in turn came to respect the open, friendly nature of the Aussie farmers and their dry sense of humour and he quickly learnt to smile when they referred to him as Fritz, Kraut or Kaiser.

It was a different story when the locals asked him to fill in for the rugby league team on Sunday because of injuries to the local lads. He could not understand why the ball wasn't round and why he had to carry it in his hands instead of kicking it along the ground. After being flattened in a pile driving tackle early in the match he went to Sandy McIntosh, the captain, to ask what he should do.

"When I hand you the bloody ball, Kaiser, I want you to run like a wild mallee bull straight over the top of those bastards and don't stop until you put it on the ground next to those posts at the other end. Ya don't have to do nothin' else. Ya got that?"

Oscar quickly got the message that it was like a medieval battle where opposing armies ran at each other until there was only one left standing and then everybody went to the local watering hole to celebrate.

He worked his way from town to town until he came to Gubba Creek where he agreed to do the farm work for the recently widowed Mary Higgins in return for food and lodgings. He had to sleep on the open verandah because Mary and her two young children occupied the two bedrooms.

Mary appreciated his hard work, his willingness to play with the children after work and his intelligent worldliness that was so different to the other local young men in town. He in turn liked her home cooking, her strong personality and her good sense of humour. The two of them would often sit for hours in the evening discussing any topic that came to mind, enjoying each other's company. In fact, after the first twelve months they were living more like a family unit, even though marriage had never been discussed.

On one Saturday afternoon, in the Commercial pub, Oscar was having a yarn with Andy Jackson, Clarrie Morrison and Taffy Edwards.

"I don't know what we're gonna do, now that ole Rusty, the dunny man, got killed in that truck accident last week, but we'll have to do somethin' soon or we'll all be in the poo," said Andy.

Andy was acting as the unofficial leader of the senior men who generally looked after town matters and made decisions without having a formal council. The town wasn't big enough for that.

"What seems to be the problem?" asked Oscar, sipping slowly on a pint of beer.

"Well, Rusty was the sano man in town, and there's no one to do that job now that he's gone. Most of the men in town will just have to look after their own cans, but we're worried about the widows and the old folk," said Clarrie.

Oscar asked lots of questions.

"How much do you get paid? How often have you got to empty the cans? Where do you take it? How do you stop the smell? How do you clean the pans? What happens when someone's sitting on the jerry can when you want to empty it? What do you do when the local Show is on in town and there're lots of extra people in town? What about the footy matches and the dances? Did Rusty have to do them as well?"

The men took their time to explain the finer points of sanitary collection and disposal and what happened in matters of high hygiene.

Oscar finished his beer and went home to discuss an idea with Mary. If he hooked up old Claude, the Clydesdale horse to the big dray, he could fit twenty cans on the back and he could do the whole town in two days. That would supplement the meagre returns from the farm."

"Then what?" asked Mary.

"What do you mean?"

"Where would you put it? All that poo. You know what I'm talking about. How could you put up with the smell? What about your clothes. You don't think I'm going to wash them, do you?"

"Don't worry love. I'll plough it all into the bottom paddock away from the homestead. No problem. It'll enrich that hard clay," replied Oscar with confidence.

Understandably it took a lot to convince Mary, but finally she agreed to a trial period. They had lots of expenses with little hope of paying for them from the meagre cropping on their poor farm.

The town elders were ecstatic with the news and organised an article in the Gubba Gazette to announce the times and fees for the new sano service. At first, Oscar was very slow and it took Claude, the horse, some time to get used to the stop, start nature of what he was supposed to do. But after a few months, Claude stopped at every house without Oscar even touching the reins. It was all done by whistle. Even the local dogs became friendly and welcomed the cart with a smile and a wag of the tail.

Young children liked Oscar and Claude and would follow them to the end of their street, much to the disgust of their mothers who did not want their children being seen following the sano cart around town. Often the kids would give a piece of carrot or apple to Claude and pat him on the neck. He, like Oscar, was a gentle giant and liked by everyone. Everyone knew that Oscar was a wonderful person who had a calming influence on the children. He would take time to discuss their problems or just talk about school, their behaviour or sport or world affairs or anything else that came to mind.

Oscar knew more about people's business than most knew about themselves. If there was a problem in one house, he knew of someone else in town who could help. He kept an eye on the old folk and organised help when they were short of wood, needed a lift to the doctor or had some rubbish to be taken away. He would always leave an extra can if he knew there were visitors in that house that week. If someone was short of cash they were allowed to pay later when things improved. Nothing was ever written down but nobody let him down.

Oscar's big smile and friendly conversations were always welcome, especially by the housewives who were stuck in the house for most days. They looked forward to having a few words with him to break the daily boredom. He knew when people were away and kept an eye on the house and questioned anyone who might go near the property in their absence. He would often arrive home with a cake, some date scones or biscuits as a present from some grateful person.

"Which one of your girlfriends have you been seeing this morning?" teased Mary on numerous such occasions.

Mary, Oscar and the children became very much involved in the town, especially with sport where they helped with coaching and fund raising. They had some very close friends, especially in the younger sporting group but, because of Oscar's work on the sano cart, they were rarely invited out for dinner, except of course to the town elders' houses, in gratitude for the work he was doing.

There were a few people however, like Mrs Bates, the wife of the bank manager, who would not even be seen in the back yard while Oscar was changing their pan in the outside dunny. Having come from upper class Melbourne, she found the whole toilet business disgusting, and would not be seen passing the time of day with Oscar or any member of the family.

One Wednesday morning as Oscar and Claude were clearing the outhouses down the lane behind the Commercial hotel, and the houses along Cypress Street, a shining black Wolseley car swung suddenly around the corner, much too fast. It hit Claude the Clydesdale broadside. Then it bumped Oscar into the gutter before coming to a stop under the broken wheel of the cart. The contents of three sanitary cans that had landed on top of the car dribbled slowly over the windscreen and bonnet and down the doors.

Mrs Bates, in her best finery, leapt from the car screaming at Oscar while frantically trying to wipe the brown stains from the white satin pleats of her best dress. The pitch and volume of her voice increased as she realised that her only escape from her embarrassment was by walking along the gutter that was now filling with the stinking ooze.

"Out of my way you dirty, disgusting, filthy man. You'll pay for this. My husband will see that you never work in this town again," screeched Mrs Bates at Oscar who was lying in the gutter in agony.

Oscar had no time to deal with Mrs Bate's tantrums. He was more concerned with his broken leg, and as he looked at poor Claude, who lay in a tangled heap of harness and dray in the gutter, he saw that the horse was barely breathing.

People came running from the nearby houses. Young Curly Wright and Jacko Jackson were driving past when the accident happened. They stopped and helped Oscar. Others found some cans of phenol to pour over the mess as a disinfectant.

Stinky Smith and his mates, Rocky, Timber and Bluey arrived with a truck load of sawdust from the timber mill. Stinky walked through the slush to cover as much as possible of the slime.

Rowdy Harris tapped Oscar on the shoulder. "I'm sorry mate but I'll have to put Claude down. He's badly injured. He's too far gone and it would be too cruel to keep him like that."

"Okay," said Oscar. "Do what you have to do. I don't want him to suffer."

Harry and Jacko took Oscar to Doc Martin's surgery, but his wife said they would have to wait for an hour because the Doc was playing an important bowls match, and she wouldn't call him back early just for a broken leg.

The next day Andy, Clarrie and Taffy met at the pub to organise a temporary sanitary can roster for the old people and widows, but decided that the others in town would have to look after their own cans until Oscar was better and could get another cart. They asked Josie at the telephone exchange to let everyone know of the temporary arrangements.

At eleven the next morning, the public bar doors to the Commercial swung open in advance of a very angry Mrs Bates demanding to speak to the town elders who, at that stage, hadn't yet had time to take their first sip of cool ale before discussing the important matters of hygiene in the town. Having got the full attention of the few drinkers in the bar she began her tirade.

"I am going to sue this town and you three men for putting me in this situation. You will have to pay for the damage to my car. I'll also need new outfits from my tailors in Melbourne and I'll need compensation for the pain and trauma I have suffered. Furthermore, my husband is a gentleman in this town and cannot be expected to empty the sanitary can. He is the bank manager as you very well know. Bank managers don't have to stoop to the lowest levels of society. It is beneath contempt to ask such a thing of a gentleman. He could not lose face and dignity in those circumstances. Now get someone else to do that job and hop to it; the can is full. I want it done by lunchtime."

"Madam," drawled Clarrie, taking a long drag on his limp greyhound cigarette as he turned slowly until he looked Mrs Bates straight in the eye. "When you ran into that cart yesterday one thing should have been very bloody obvious. When the can that Oscar picked up from your place spilt into the gutter, your shit and everyone else's looked and smelt exactly the same, you couldn't pick one from the other. So, like everyone else, you and your husband can empty your own can until Oscar is fit enough to start work again. I don't care whether you wipe your arse on the Melbourne Age, a torn-up telephone book or a gum leaf. What comes out is still big, brown and it stinks, just like what comes out of all of the rest of us country hicks. There are a lot of old and sick people in town who need our help before you. Now get off before I give you a shovel to clean up the gutter where you crashed your car."

Mrs Bates stormed out the door with such force it almost came off its hinges. She strode off to complain to her husband.

Ten minutes later, Edgar Bates arrived at the Commercial Hotel. He asked Clarrie if they could have a private conversation in the back room next to the saloon bar. After listening politely to Edgar's tale of woe, and his concern for the bank's image and that of his wife and himself, Clarrie, in his own slow dry manner, summed up the main issues fairly clearly.

"Let's put it this way, Edgar. Your wife caused the accident. Oscar has lost his horse and cart and can't work until his leg heals. He'll never walk the same again. The people in this town are pretty shitty about this, and many of them want to take their business to the other banks. Some were gunna throw your missus into the sheep dip down at the yards, or tar and feather her at the back of the Shell depot. But being the gentleman that I am, Edgar, I put a stop to that nonsense, just for you. I prevailed on the boys to use restraint until I had sorted out this matter. It was the least I could do for a man of your standing."

Clarrie paused, turned his head to spit out the window, and gave time for that comment to sink in before continuing. "Now hear this, Edgar. Now that your missus killed Claude, poor Oscar will need a good truck when he gets back on the job, and I happen to know that Paddy Doyle has one for sale. So, you and your missus and the bank better get off your arses, and get your bloody heads together to find a way to buy that truck. When that happens, I might be able to keep the dogs and the blokes in this town on the leash. I'll give you till the end of the week. Take it or leave it Edgar, and by the way, nobody is going to empty your can."

When Edgar told his wife she threw a tantrum that would have put a pen full of wild boars to shame. "That's blackmail. I won't be dictated to by a pack of country hicks. You go and tell them, Edgar. Get someone to empty those cans; now."

Over the next three weeks Edgar waited until Mrs Bates went to her church Fellowship meetings. He used that opportunity to drive out to a dirt track off Sandy Creek Road to empty his dunny can into an erosion gully. He had asked the junior clerk in the bank to do it for him but he refused because he was Andy Jackson's son and he was more frightened of his father than old man Bates.

Edgar noticed that some customers were already withdrawing their deposits and transferring their accounts to the other banks. He had no desire to explain to head office why this was happening. That night he gave his wife an ultimatum; either they finance the new truck or he would have to resign, and he could never work for the bank again.

On the following Saturday the big day arrived. Almost everyone in town was in the main street in front of the Commercial pub. Mary and the kids drove Oscar along the street in the sulky to resounding cheers from one and all. There to meet them was a welcoming committee of Andy, Clarrie, Taffy and Mister and Missus Bates.

"Oscar," said Andy, after Oscar had stepped down from the sulky and leaned against the verandah post for support. "It's so good to see you on your feet again and ready to get back to work. The town's been in a stinkin' mess since you had your accident. I'm glad that's now over and I'm goin' to ask Mrs Bates, on behalf of the bank, to make a presentation."

He turned. "Mrs Bates, over to you."

Mrs Bates, dressed in her neatly ironed navy silk coat dress, white leather gloves and a white straw Panama hat with a rose in front, stepped forward nervously. She paused to gain her composure before drawing herself to her full height, and announced. "Mr Collins; on behalf of my husband and I, and the good auspices of the Commercial Bank, which has always been at the forefront in assisting the community of Gubba Creek, I would like to present you with the keys to this vehicle, and I'm so glad to see you are ready to go back to work again."

At that moment Rowdy Harris blasted some badly off-key notes from an old bugle. All the town's folk, lined along the footpath outside the hotel, cheered in unison.

"Good on ya Rowdy," called Stinger Ray. "that'll shake the bloody dust out of the trees. Give us the Last Post, mate."

There was another round of cheers.

Clarrie and Taffy then stepped forward. They walked over to the truck with the cabin covered in a large stained tarpaulin. They pulled back the big tarp to reveal a shiny, newly painted truck. As the canvas came off the cabin and slid to the ground everyone could clearly see on the door, printed in large red letters:

O D Cologne
Hygiene engineer
Gubba Creek

Oscar walked up to Mrs Bates and gave her a big hug and a kiss and thanked her and her husband for their kind thoughts and generosity. Mrs Bates shuddered and tried to retreat but Oscar's arms held her tight. She wondered how quickly she could get home to change her clothes and have a bath. And to make matters worse, this touching scene was captured on camera for the front page of the next Gubba Gazette.

To add insult to injury, the men at the garage had painted some extra words on the door of the truck as a permanent reminder of Missus Bates' association with the sanitary service of Gubba Creek.

Kindly Presented to Gubba Creek
by Mrs Rosemary Bates.

Cat Licks and Prods

Into Gubba Creek station shuddered the old steam engine, belching a cloud of exhaustion before settling back into quiet puffs of steam as it relaxed after its long overnight journey. Unfolding himself slowly through the red peeled-paint open door of the old dog box carriage at the back of the train, was the tall gangly frame of an English gentleman in a Harris tweed suit, highly polished shoes and his collar in reverse. He pulled his neat felt hat low as he looked into the bright sun.

The Reverend Gordon West, fresh from the green hills of Kent in England, had arrived to take up his mission to bring God's good works to the antipodean heathens of Gubba Creek. It was his first appointment in this strange new land.

The heat penetrated deeply into the heavy woollen cloth. Perspiration irritated his coal-dust-stained collar and flies penetrated every facial orifice as he surveyed the untidy, weed strewn railway yard between him and the main street. The shop verandahs drooped like heavy lids protecting their stained windows; the eyes into the dusty shop interiors. A lone kelpie dog slowly peed on the telephone post leaning at an odd angle beside the laneway.

There was little activity in town except at the silos where a line of trucks waited to unload their bags of wheat. Reverend West was already starting to question why he had followed his uncle's advice to leave war torn England to carry God's word to the colonies at the other end of the earth.

"I say, good chappie," he called to the young railway attendant leaning against the door frame, chewing his fingernails, "there don't appear to be many people in town today."

"Nah." drawled Dusty Jackson, lips barely moving, his forefinger moving slowly across his face to keep the flies from his eyes. "Well, it's like this, ya see, if you get me drift. People don't come to Gubba Creek to get to somewhere else. There's no great crowd of visitors rushin' about like flies around a dead sheep's carcass, are there? Like; it's the end of the line, can't ya see. There's no other reason ta be here. Do you git what I mean, eh?"

Dusty hitched his trousers and wiped his nose on his sleeve.

"Would you be so kind as to direct me to the church?" asked the man of the cloth.

"Which one?" questioned Dusty. "The Cat Licks are up on the hill over there. All of the Prods are down on the flats across the town. Hey, you must be the new Reverend. Chuck ya bags on Clarrie's truck over there. He'll take you up to the church."

The new minister arrived at the two-storey weatherboard house with the overgrown garden in front and a faded, disintegrating rectory sign near the front steps. Mrs Simpson, in her finest floral dress, starched to impress, and with all the gush and flourish she could muster, welcomed the new minister to the rectory and ushered him into the lounge for tea and scones.

131

She poured a glass of cool water and placed her hand confidently on his arm. "I've left the Reverend Lewis' notes for you in your study. He has given you a summary of your duties and the nature of the church's district. He was such a wonderful, wonderful, caring man. He was kind and loving to everyone. I don't know why he was taken away so quickly. They must have wanted him for higher duties. We will miss him so dearly," she said.

Gordon West resisted the logical response. He remembered his Bishop's explanation of why Lewis had been hastily moved to another state. It was because of his affair with this married woman who was now preening herself in front of him. Very clearly embedded in his mind was his Grace's explanation about the woman's husband's threat to castrate Lewis if he could get hold of him. His advice to West was to keep his own primeval urges under control in Gubba Creek.

"Your first duty," said Mrs Simpson, "will be tomorrow afternoon at the local school where you will take the combined Protestant scripture. The Catholics run their own. They won't have anything to do with us."

The following afternoon, the reverend gentleman paid his respects to the school principal before proceeding to Room 4 where he surveyed with a sinking heart a mixed bag of God's Protestant darlings; Anglicans, Presbyterians, Methodists, a couple of Lutherans, Baptists and a few others who didn't know or seem to care which denomination they subscribed to. Some were neatly dressed and well groomed, but most had no shoes, and the patches held their clothing together.

"Good afternoon children, I am Canon West, your new minister. I'm new here, so I would like you to tell me about yourselves. Tell me about your families and this town. I would like to get to know you."

"Are you really a cannon? Do you shoot sinners?" asked Blinky Hughes, eyes flicking nervously from side to side. "Do you carry big guns under that white dress you wear on Sundays?"

"If you're Cannon West, are you the brother of Shotgun South?" chortled Snowy Mitchell, picking the wax from his ear.

"Have ya ever seen God? What's he look like? Does he really wear a dress like a shiela?" asked Rowdy Moffatt.

"Are you married? Did ya bring the missus with ya, or are ya gunna live with Mrs Simpson?" asked Sammy Butcher.

The Reverend was stunned at the open friendliness and the uninhibited, unsophisticated directness of these children. It was certainly not like the Great Public Schools of Kent and the very proper manners of English students with whom he was familiar.

Jumper Jones put up his hand. "Why don't the Cat Licks eat meat on Fridays? They say it's a sin. Will we die if we have snags and t'marter sauce on Friday? Will we?"

Dasher Stephenson stopped scratching his long curly hair and picking the hardened scab on his knee long enough to slowly make a statement of note.

"Me ole man says it's useless goin' to church. He says that the road from our farm into town is so rough and corrugated that ya git the devil shaken out of ya on the way into town to church and Christ shaken out of ya on the way back. Be the time ya gits home, ya no better orf. Waste of bloody time goin' there in the first place.

Ya better orf spending that time shootin' rabbits. At least there's something to show for it after."

Dasher leaned back with a big sigh, exhausted from all that talking.

"They say that the old church house is haunted," said Jacko. "Is there a holy ghost in the bedroom?"

"Na," said Harry. "That was bloody old Mad Mollie. She was the housekeeper who jumped off the balcony and killed 'erself."

Young Cracker Dunlop jumped out from behind his desk and ran around the room with arms outstretched. "Whooooooooo; Whooooooooo; Whooooooooo. I am the Holy Ghost. Whooooooooo; Whooooooooo."

"Sit down, Cracker," snapped his sister, Annabelle. "Mr West is trying to teach us about religion. Sit down. Shut up and behave yourself or Mum will give you a ghost of a hiding when ya git home."

"Why can't you marry a Cat Lick shiela?" asked Dutchy Holland. "I'd like to go out with Kathleen O'Sullivan but her old man won't let her talk to me. He said he'd shoot me if I sat next to her at the flicks on Satdee arvo."

"Sir, sir, sir, sir," pleaded Millicent Anderson, pushing up her hand, trying desperately to get a word in above the banter and laughter of the boys. "Is it true that you drink the blood of Christ from that silver cup on Sunday?"

"Don't be a silly billy, Milly," said Splinter Thompson, "That's not blood. That's plonk, ya know. It's Sherry. Ya buy it down the pub. Why do you think old Metho Morris and Ding Dong

Bell go to church on Sunday? The minister has to drag the cup away from their mouths. It's their free booze on Sunday."

As the Reverend was considering how he might explain the spiritual complexities of the holy communion, his thoughts were shattered by the sharp peeling of the bell signalling the end of the school day. He barely got through a final blessing before there was an explosion of pent-up energy from the sweaty bodies bursting through the door into the dusty playground to mix with an equally exuberant herd of Catholic youth from the next room running towards the gate. Across the road was the hard overgrown patch of clay, loosely referred to as the local recreation ground. It was the location of all major sporting events in the district.

"Hey, Paddy, Mick, you're on my team this arvo. We'll be the Bradmans and Andy's team are the Poms," said Dutchy.

Red McQuade shouted. "Me and Doyley want to be on Andy's team. We'll thrash Dutchy's mob."

The boys quickly split into two competing teams for the daily competition. The match was as serious as a full test match at the Sydney Cricket Ground. A forty-four-gallon drum at one end and some pickets from the school fence at the other, marked the length of the pitch.

Reverend Gordon West stood on the verandah of the school to watch and learn more of the local customs, the nature of his new flock, and how this ecumenical union of Protestants and Catholics on the recreation ground might pan out. How could it possibly compare to the hallowed turf of England, he thought.

Everything went well until precisely 4 o'clock. There was a loud piercing voice accompanied by a bell and the constant yapping

135

of a small Pomeranian dog coming from the small weatherboard house on the northern side of the oval. Standing at the front gate was Miss O'Flaherty, an over proportioned spinster in a shapeless dark blue dress that covered all but her bloated florid face, her tightly knotted hair and her pudgy hands that held an overweight cat.

Talk in the town was that the dog and cat had been specially trained to attack Protestants. There were grown men who would walk on the other side of the road to avoid confrontations with those little beasts and the protestations of Miss O'Flaherty.

Miss O'Flaherty was the self-appointed teacher of the catechism and the supervisor of Catholic values and ideals in the town and she nurtured a hatred of the 'heathen' Protestants. She took boys and girls in separate classes after school. There was no way she would have Spud Murphy and Mary Mallone distracted from God's word by being together in the same room at the same time in her house.

Father Murphy, the local priest, was very happy with this arrangement as he had no particular desire to force the catechism into unwilling young minds. His felt his time was far better spent ministering to those poor lost souls who gathered daily in the public bars at the Railway, Commercial and the Great Northern hotels, especially when those poor souls tried to buy their way to heaven by paying for the Priest's drinks.

"Boys, come here right now, this minute," snapped Miss O'Flaherty. "Hurry on, I don't have all day to waste while you play your stupid games. Get away from those heathen prods. Murphy, Sullivan, Doyle, come here now. God waits for nobody."

Splinter shouted at the Catholic boys as they walked away. "Gawn, you Cat Licks. Ol' Farty's got the catty kissies for you. Gawn, go kiss your catty, catty kisses. Git down on your knees and kiss the pussy."

As he ran to the house, Paddy turned and shouted over his shoulder. "You bloody Prods. You aren't even Christians. You'll all go to hell."

Splinter threw a paddy melon in his direction. "You'll get hell if you don't run over to old O'Farty now. That mongrel pup will bite your bloody leg off."

"I'm gunna git you after," shouted Red O"Farrell.

Dutchy chimed in. "Ya couldn't git yourself in ya own backyard on a sunny day so ya couldn't git me. Ya couldn't fight ya way out of a dust storm without ya big sister holding ya hand."

Bluey Doyle picked up a large clod and threw it at Smiley Morris. This was a signal for a bombardment of clods and overripe paddy melons being hurled from both directions like a hail of spears and arrows in a battle between the Crusaders and the infidels. Terry copped a clod on the ear. Andy got a melon in the face where it split and slowly slid down the front of his shirt. This prompted several more barrages of soft and hard missiles.

This weekly ritual did much for the propagation of the rambling paddy melons in the district but very little for religious tolerance.

"I'll bloody git you after, Doyle," shouted Smiley, as the Catholics retreated into the safety of Miss O'Flaherty's ample religious protectorate.

"You and whose army," retorted Bluey.

While the Catholic boys were inside, the Protestants played a game of touch football using an ancient misshapen piece of leather held together by numerous stitches of string punched through its gaping seams. At times the game got over vigorous when the boys hit the dust. Bleeding knees and noses were testament to the intensity of the contest.

At 4.30 sharp, there were shouts and whoopees as the Catholic boys rushed out onto the dusty paddock again.

"Hey Doyley," shouted Smiley Morris. "You're on my side this time. We're the Bradmans and Murph can be the Poms with Andrew for a change."

Without much hesitation the two groups came together and then broke up into two different teams for the next test match. The earlier battles were forgotten in the rush to score runs or bowl out the other side before sunset.

About an hour later, as the setting sun turned the dust haze into a glowing ball of fire, the boys called a halt to the match and walked home; Cat Licks and Prods together, arms around each other, mates, friends; telling jokes and taking the mickey out of each other at every opportunity.

The Reverend Gordon West, who had stood on the school verandah all afternoon, watching the tribal pursuits of these boys on that barren, dusty recreation ground, walked slowly back to the rectory.

He shook his head slowly from side to side, deep in thought, as he tried to come to terms with his experiences on his first day at Gubba Creek; this remote outpost of God's Kingdom. By the time he reached the sanctuary of the Rectory, he could come to only one conclusion; God, in this part of his world, most certainly moved in mysterious ways.

Nineteen Forty-Two

Hey Mum, hey Mum, the Japs are comin'
They're going to bayonet and eat us kids
And rape all the women.
It said so on the poster in the dunny in the park.
We've all got to join up.
Hey Mum what's rape?
Oh, do be quiet Johnny, let me think
Now go next door to Mrs Bruce
And borrow two ounces of butter.
I'll pay her back on ration day.
I need to cook a birthday cake for Sarah.
Now be off with you, that's a good boy.

Hey Mum, hey Mum, there's blowies in the kitchen
I swatted ten on the table
Before they were able
To get to the roast and vegies.
Hey Mum, tell the Japs if they come to Australia
We'll put the blowies down their pants

And the maggots will eat their guts out
And their trousers will hang down like dags on their bum.
Oh, do be quiet Johnny, let me think.
Go down the back and cut some wood for the copper
I've got a lot of washing to do.
Now be off with you. That's a good boy.

Hey Mum, hey Mum, the locusts are comin'
They're swarmin' across the yard.
I'll get the green things off the line
And me trousers off the verandah.
Hey Mum, tell those Japs if they come here
The locusts will eat their clothes
The sun will burn their skin off and the frost
Will freeze 'em solid.
Oh, do be quiet Johnny, let me think.
Go to the store to get me some spuds
And tell old Franklin from me
That I'll have his balls for breakfast
If he slips in a rotten one, he'll see.
Now be off with you. That's a good boy.

Hey Mum, hey Mum, the dust storm is comin'
It's rollin' over the paddocks, somethin' scary.
Get the kids to close the winders an' doors
And cover the tables and chairs.
Hey Mum, tell the Japs if they come
They'll have to climb that big red mountain

141

And when they fall, they'll be kicked by the roos
And choked to death by the dust.
Oh, do be quiet Johnny, let me think.
Go to the ice works and get me a block
And don't dawdle on the way
I want to keep that meat cool in the chest
Now be off with you. That's a good boy.

Hey Mum, hey Mum, the rats are in the shed
They're eatin' all the chook feed
They're crawlin' up the lemon tree and jumping on the roof
They'll be comin' down the chimney and chewin' at our feet.
Hey Mum, tell the Japs if they come
Our rats are as big as bears
And kick like a big red kangaroo
 That should give 'em a scare.
Oh, do be quiet Johnny, let me think.
Go change Sarah's nappy, son,
Give it a rinse in the yard
Put it in the bucket by the copper
 Now be off with you. That's a good boy.

Hey Mum, hey Mum, there's drops of water fallin'.
We're goin' to have a storm
Look at the big red spots on me chest
Me singlet's got the measles.
Hey Mum, tell those Japs when they come
We'll tackle 'em in the mud

And we'll turn their yella faces
Into big red speckled spuds.
Oh, do be quiet Johnny, let me think.
Run down to O D Cologne
That big nice sano man
And ask him to come and empty the can
Cause it's overflowin' again.
Now be off with you. That's a good boy.

Oh Bert, Oh Bert, where are you
When I need you most of all.
I know you're in New Guinea
Cause you wrote it under the stamp
On the envelope so
the censor couldn't find it.
But it's getting' hard to cope, Bert
And the kids do miss you so.
Johnny, come here to Mum
Give me a great big kiss and a hug
I love you so much; you great big lug.
Aw gees Mum, not one of those big sloppy ones
Not in front of the others
It's so embarrassin'.

The Canopy

It was her most prized possession, something she had worked for over the years. It was a gem among her many other valuables. It was purchased as a reward for her hard work and dedication to the family business. It was a canopy bed, but not just any canopy bed.

This was a Californian, Colonial, Genuine, Mahogany, Canopy bed imported from the United States at considerable expense. There it stood, in all its majesty, against the wall opposite the windows. It was the centrepiece of the bedroom that also featured an antique chest of drawers, wardrobes and a dressing table acquired over the years from various clearing sales of well-known large properties in the district.

The exquisitely turned four posts supported a solid, highly polished mahogany canopy from which hung two mosquito nets, drawn back by midnight blue satin ribbons. The brocaded, gold edged satin bed cover, was neatly folded under the pillows and fell precisely to one inch from the floor. It completed the image of rock-solid quality and class. It would have been easy to believe that the whole bedroom was set up as an exhibition rather than for the practical reality of a romp, slap and tickle in the dark or a lazy lay in on Sunday morning while spilling toast crumbs onto the sheets.

While this bed was Susan's most valuable acquisition, it was in keeping with the rest of the house. The building was a solid, double brick Australian Colonial dwelling with extensive verandahs, surrounded by lawns, pepper trees and oleanders for shade and colour. The other rooms were decorated with quality antique furniture, coordinated with lamps and objects d'art that reflected her taste for good design and fashion.

Susan Jones, the owner of this fine piece of furniture, was born and bred in Gubba Creek, the only child of Harold and Margaret Jennings. Susan's father came to town after the Great War and set himself up as a mechanic in an old tin shed at the back of the Co-Op Store. Because he was a fitter and turner by trade, he was able to manufacture bits and pieces to get the job done when spare parts were as scarce as hens' teeth. Farmers, in particular, valued his ability and willingness to get their machinery going under all circumstances. His ingenuity and hard work paid off and he eventually established himself in the main street in new premises in the name of 'Gubba Creek Automotives and Machinery'.

Susan loved her parents and, as a child, would spend every minute of her spare time in the garage helping out. Her father taught her how to strip and recondition motors, and by the time she reached her teens she was as good as any of the mechanics. She might not have had the physical strength of the men, but more than made up for that with her intelligence, wit, wisdom and work ethic.

She also quickly came to terms with the intricacies of running the business, guided by her talented mother, who carried the bulk of that responsibility. To make her mark in a man's town like Gubba Creek and in a man's business such as car mechanics, was no mean feat. She had to shake off the pretty girl in blond curls image to the point where she could bargain with the hard men of the district; those who always wanted things done yesterday for the smallest payment that might, or might not, be paid after the next harvest.

When Susan was in her late teens her father took on an apprentice, Andy Jones. He was a tall, friendly, athletic, raw boned young man with a deep love of cars and what made them tick. His other love was sport and he showed considerable talent for all sports. He had no shortage of girls wanting his attention and he was always in demand at the local dances and balls, but his shyness and immaturity held him in reserve and at arms' length from his admirers. Andy soon proved to Harold that he was a worthy worker, one to be kept on in the garage at all costs.

At first, Susan was a little jealous of Andy. She felt that Andy was treated more like the son her father didn't have, but so dearly wanted, to eventually take over the business. Andy, at first, kept his distance from Susan. He didn't want to be seen being fresh with the boss's daughter. His apprenticeship was the most important thing in his life.

Gradually however, as they leaned together over warm bonnets and lay together under the cars next to hot exhausts, the ice started to melt. Touches lingered. Smiles broadened. Jokes were shared and challenges accepted. Although she would not admit it, Susan would walk past the Recreation Ground on the weekend to catch a glimpse of Andy playing football.

"Hey, Susan and Andy, come in here," shouted Harold one day. "I've done my knee in and I want you two to go out to old Matt Hagan's farm at Sandy Creek and pick up his tractor. Take the ramps and chains. It'll take the two of you to guide it onto the truck and chain it down. Now don't be long, old Matt wants it fixed and back tomorrow."

Susan drove the truck on the way out to Matt's, but at the ten mile peg she suddenly took a turn up Lambing Lane and off the track into the long grass beside the creek. She walked around the truck, opened the other door, took hold of Andy's collar, dragged him out and pushed him down into the grass under the tree.

Had it been summer and had the grass been dry, they would have started a bushfire. Even the frilled neck lizard and the red bellied black snake stayed perfectly still behind the trees, not wanting to become entangled in this strange human ritual playing out in front of them. Dandelions and locusts were scattered in all directions. When the breeze eventually subsided, they dusted each other off and, with some embarrassment, helped each other sort out the twisted heap of clothes on the ground.

Five weeks after this little rural excursion, Susan asked Andy to go for a walk at lunch time.

"Andy, listen to me carefully," she said soberly. "I've something important to tell you. I think, in fact, I'm pretty sure, I'm certain that I'm pregnant. What do you think we should do?"

"There's only one thing to do," replied Andy. "We'll get married. I couldn't think of nothing I'd like more. What do you think, eh?"

Three weeks later, Andy and Susan had one of the biggest weddings in the district. It seemed the whole town was there. Harold and Margaret quickly got over their initial shock, and by the time the premature baby came along they were ecstatic. The pair lived with her parents until Michael was born. Then they moved into an old house down the street. Two years later, Julie was born and they could not have been happier.

Over the next twenty years success built on success, from poor to rich, from common folk to social recognition, from enthusiastic youngsters to mature parents.

After the death of her parents, Susan took over the running of the business, expanding it to include a car and truck sales yard and a farm machinery section.

"We Sell It, We Service It and We Buy It Back." was their motto. It was so successful that all other competition left town or went broke. Andy had nothing to do with the management. He was the best mechanic in town but had no head for business. Susan was the brains behind every move and she had a good understanding of, and compassion for the trials and tribulations of the farming community, and was well respected by everyone in town.

When the children enrolled in private schools and then later left home to take on studies at university, Susan became more involved in community affairs. She was President of the local CWA, secretary of the Show Society, member of the Church Auxiliary and the Red Cross. On at least three days in every week, she attended some meeting or other to organise a ball, dance, fete, parade, ceremony or award.

She and Margaret Morris, wife of the local Sergeant of Police were the people who got things done in town. On most days they were inseparable. On every day she spent some time in the garage keeping a careful eye on the business. Andy, on the other hand, spent most of his spare time with sport, as a coach of the local football and cricket teams where he had lots of success in district competitions.

With the growth of the business, Susan could afford the better things in life. She built the new big house and filled it with the antique furniture. She had membership of the best clubs. She took holidays in the top hotels in the cities, shopping sprees in town with the girls, a new Oldsmobile, and of course, the purchase of those things she had always dreamed of, such as the Californian, colonial, genuine mahogany canopy bed with all the trimmings.

Andy, on the other hand, was not fussed by all the finery. He went along with Susan's wishes because, let's face it, she was the one making the money, and it was better than living in the old rusty tin shed his parents had when he was a boy. Although he wouldn't say anything, he was probably a little jealous of Susan and her ability to get things done and make money. He much preferred getting his kicks in the sporting fields and having a drink with the boys after work and on the weekends.

The town saw them as the perfect couple. Susan and Andy were recognised for their own abilities and achievements. But, behind the public image, the cells in their batteries were no longer giving off the same spark as they did in those halcyon days of their youth when their athletic vigour was as good in the bedroom as it was on the playing field. These days, the crusting on their personal battery leads reduced the spark to the point where it would hardly light a candle.

"I see Trixie Walsh came to see you yesterday," said Margaret Morris to Susan on the way to their CWA meeting. "I saw her poodle tied up at your side door as I drove past."

"No. She must have missed me. I was in the garage most of the day doing the stock taking and getting the tax papers in order," replied Susan. "I wonder what she wanted from me. I'll catch up with her later in the week."

Margaret leaned forward across the dash to look more directly at Susan. "Of course, she might have been there talking to Andy. His truck was out the front at the time. He was probably there having his lunch. It was about that time of day. I'd keep a careful eye on that Trixie, if I was you, Susan. Since she lost her husband Tommy, she's been on the loose looking for any pair of pants to climb into. I wouldn't trust her as far as I'd kick her."

That night, after her meetings, Susan decided to question Andy about Trixie's visit the day before.

Andy seemed a little startled but took another sip from his bottle of beer.

"Yeah, while I was having lunch, Trixie dropped in while she was out walking her dog and she saw my truck out front. She's been having some trouble with her car, and because Tommy's now passed on, there's nobody to do the routine maintenance. I called in on the way back to work and fixed it. It was only a dirty carby. It only took me five minutes. Nothin' to it really," replied Andy with not a shadow crossing his honest face.

On two more occasions over the next few weeks, other friends of Susan mentioned that they had seen Trixie visit her at home at lunch time. Susan knew that she had not been home on those days. Because Andy normally went home for lunch, she questioned him again about Trixie's visits and he always gave a simple explanation.

"Trixie is very worried about young Harry, who hasn't got over the death of his father yet. She's asked me to talk to him and give him support because he's in my junior football team. I said I'd help if I could. She calls in every now and then to check how things are going. Harry's starting to settle down now. He's a good kid who needs a bit of help over a rough patch. She came around again the other day to ask me if I could do a service on their diesel generator. It was cutting out."

Susan trusted Andy at first, but then became suspicious. On some days when she came home, she found the gold edged, brocaded bed cover on the canopy bed not exactly as it was when she left that morning...one inch from the floor on all sides. Those days always coincided with more sightings of Trixie walking her poodle at their end of town.

Susan had an idea. One morning before heading to work she came in from the shed carrying a tool box into the bedroom.

"What are you doing with the tool box love?" inquired Andy "Is there anything I can do for you?"

"No thanks Andy, darling, I'm just tightening up some bolts on our bed. It's developed a bit of a squeak lately and it's driving me mad. It keeps me awake at night. One of the joints must be loose. You know how fussy I am about things like this. You sleep like a log. You wouldn't even hear it."

"I'll do it for you love," said Andy.

"I don't need your help, darling. I can do it myself. I'm still handy with the shifter and screwdriver you know. Oh, and, by the way, I'm going to be busy all day with meetings. There's CWA all morning, then lunch at Margaret's, then all afternoon we are organising the Show Ball at the School of Arts. I won't be home 'til six tonight. I've left some lunch in the fridge for you. Have a great day, darling."

At lunch time, after they had closed business at the CWA meeting, Susan and Margaret drove towards the police station but Susan stopped, turned the car around and headed back the other way.

"Margaret, I forgot the boxes of decorations for the ball. Would you mind coming back home with me and help me load them into the car?"

"Sure, no worries, let's go. There's plenty of time before we start this afternoon's meeting. After we load up at your place we can still go back to my place for lunch. I've cooked us some pies," replied Margaret.

As they went to the back door, they patted Trixie's poodle before going into the kitchen. There was nobody in there. Susan went through to the bedroom. She let forth with a piercing scream. "Margaret, get in here quickly. Give me a hand."

There was Andy, stark naked, spread-eagled, face down on the gold edged brocaded bed cover. The cross beam from one end of the highly polished mahogany bed canopy pinned him down

152

across the back of his neck. Ruffles of mosquito net covered most of his body and hung loosely over the sides of the bed.

"Quick Margaret," Susan shouted. "Give me a hand to lift this off Andy."

As they heaved the heavy canopy from Andy's neck, a pink skinned naked piglet named Trixie tried desperately to untangle herself from the netting, squealing loudly as she pushed Andy's body from on top of her. As she rushed to the door, she tried to retrieve as many garments as possible along the way. Margaret, a former nurse, quickly moved in to check Andy.

"Susan, I'm finding it difficult to get a pulse. Help me roll him over so I can get a better go at it," said Margaret.

"Is he alright? Is he still breathing?" pleaded Susan.

After a few minutes Margaret came around to take Susan in an embrace. "I'm sorry to have to tell you this Susan, but I think the canopy's broken his neck. I think it killed him. I'll ring the doctor and Jim to come down from the police station to check it out. Come out to the kitchen with me."

After a careful examination of the scene, Margaret's husband, Sergeant Jim Morris, talked to the doctor who then declared on the certificate; "Death by Misadventure".

The funeral was a great success, one of the biggest ever seen in Gubba Creek. The wake at the RSL Bowling Club went most of the night, though it was embarrassing when Charlie Tomlinson announced in a drunken stupor over the loud speaker that, when his time came, he wanted to go like Andy, in the saddle with his boots and spurs on, and his whip still flashing at the finish. Susan was

153

embarrassed by this outburst but calmed again after Dutchy took Charlie out the back for his own good.

The last anyone saw of Trixie, she was heading south at full speed, with one white poodle sucking in the air from the open window, unlikely ever to turn north again.

It can now be confirmed that old Harry Stevenson, a crippled World War I Digger who lived as a caretaker in the big shed at the back of the farm machinery yard, is now the proud owner of an exquisite Californian Colonial Genuine Mahogany Four Poster bed with gold edged brocaded cover. It is missing the canopy, which is now feeding the white ants among the wrecked cars in the yard at the back of the police station while awaiting examination as evidence.

The New Batch

It's the new school year. Well, I wonder what this new batch of kids will be like. I hope they're better than the lot we had last year. What will this incoming wave of fresh humanity add to the tired and unruly flotsam we had last year? Here I am on this first Tuesday of the school year at the end of a long hot holiday. As I look out from the school verandah across the dusty, weed strewn playground, I'm almost too scared to look. Who might come along the road today? Who will enter these gates of eternal wisdom that we call the District School? Who will come to sample what we have to offer?

The last few months of last year had few highlights worth remembering. Three boys were suspended for stealing bottles of perfume from the Co-Op store. They gave them as Christmas presents to their teacher, Miss Atkinson. The boy and girl captains were caught under the main building in a compromising situation after the farewell dance, and Timber Woods punched Mister Andrews, the football coach, for not awarding the 'Best and Fairest' to his son.

All the kids last year were a bit flighty because some of their dads had been demobbed from the war and found it hard to settle back into their old ways of caring for their family. Other families were still anxious because their dads had been sent to Japan as part of the occupation forces, with no certainty how long they would be away.

The former Principal, Mr Fogarty, the miserable old skinflint, docked me two days' pay in November because my old Austin car broke down at Sandy Creek on the way to the first test between the Aussies and the Poms. I not only missed seeing Bradman score 187 and Hassett 128 but we beat the Poms by an innings and I had to wait two days in Sandy Creek for the repairs. Cost me 50 quid and I was docked pay and never saw a single ball bowled.

I went to the city to be with my Mum and Dad at Christmas time. That was about as exciting as watching snails copulate. They never understood why I became a teacher and why I didn't follow Dad into the accounting firm. How could I tell him I've always believed that, in an open competition between an accountant and a grain of sand, the sand would win hands down every time because it would find some mates and form a beach where we could all have fun.

They pestered me why I'd want to leave the city to work in an outback country town. I couldn't convince them that far more happens in a country town in one week than happens in their sleepy little suburb in the city in a whole year.

After five days of putting up with my sister's two young brats, I was glad to travel down the coast where I booked into a Guest House on the beach. I was just starting to get cosy with this sweet young thing from Melbourne when her mum took her back

156

on the train. I felt like a born loser again, especially when the others in the Guest House from the city tended to stick together and didn't want anything to do with us country bumpkins.

Well, never mind. Here we are back to face another year at the chalk face. Surely it has to be better than last year. Look, here comes the first lot of parents and kids coming down the road now. There's Laura Briggs with her tribe. Five kids from five fathers and none of them have been her husband. When Laura went to school, she never quite reached that level of understanding where she could put N and O together to say NO!

Even Laura probably doesn't know who the real fathers are. That is of course except for young Tommy, whose red hair and freckles make him a dead ringer for Rusty Jackson. Rusty vehemently denies ever having slept with her. But Laura is a happy-go-lucky soul who loves her kids and lives with her mother who, in turn, loves all those kids and treats them as her own. Pop Briggs couldn't care less because he spends most of his time in the bush, boring wells.

Close behind Laura is an old Clydesdale horse with three kids riding on its back. Their legs stuck out like thin leather straps flapping in rhythm with the easy gait of the horse. Young Freddy Woods was at the back, holding the young twins in front, because they were starting first class today. Poor Mrs Woods. The twins are her fifteenth and sixteenth kids in the family of eighteen and there's another bun in the oven. It's a wonder she hasn't tied a knot in his old bloke.

Old Jack Woods owns a dairy and piggery just out of town on the river and we were sure that Mrs Woods had to produce a litter every year or she would end up down at Butch Edwards shop as pork chops or sausages. The locals call their farm the Timber Mill. But the kids are great and they all help out on the farm and in the house. The older girls cook up a huge pot of porridge each morning, and they all line up army fashion on the verandah to get their share. There's not a pair of shoes among them, and their clothes are hand-me-downs, with the smallest having the most and biggest patches. I reckon we could keep this school open just for the Woods and the Briggs' families alone.

"G'day, Andy. Enjoy your holiday?" I asked as Andrew Flatley, another teacher, emerged from the staff room to look over the new pupils as they entered the playground.

"Oh, not bad," replied Andrew. "I went home to help Dad in the pub. It was pretty boring most of the time except for the 6 o'clock swill when some blokes got stroppy when they couldn't get served one more time before closing. But the money I earned will help me buy a car."

Just then, Mrs Bates, wife of the new Bank Manager, arrived at the school gates in the shiny black 1937 Wolseley. She strode through the gate holding a protective hand on Jonathon, whom she had attired in a clean white shirt, blue striped tie, freshly ironed grey shorts and highly polished shoes.

Oh my goodness, that tie won't last the day, and that shirt and shoes will be western red dirt by lunchtime. All that's missing is the straw boater to make him look like the Melbourne Grammar student his mother wanted him to be. If he'd worn the boater it would be fodder for the Woods' horse by now.

Mrs Bates, in all her finery, was determined to put on a display of moneyed Melbourne, and was at pains to tell everyone that her father was a prominent merchant banker and her husband was the new manager in town. She hadn't given any thought to what her son would have to go through in his initiation into country life. Sometimes I think kids would be better off without parents.

"I have an appointment with the headmaster," she announced as she flounced up the steps. Flatley and I bow as she swept past. All we needed was for some clown on the staff like Bazza Welsh to refer to young Jonathon as "Maasterbates".

I'll give him a clip under the ear if he does. For goodness' sake, the kid's got enough to put up with his mother and father without further embarrassment from Barry's crudity.

I retreated to the men's staff room for a cup of coffee. I was just in time to hear Ken Smythe give a stern lecture to young Peter Anderson, the new young teacher who had the audacity to use Ken's exclusive fine bone porcelain cup and saucer for his early morning cup of tea.

Ken; short, balding, neatly dressed in a pin striped suit and with a shining spiked waxed moustache that quivered with tension, was the recognized elder on the staff. He demanded and got the privilege of placing his fine China cup and saucer in the left-hand corner, exactly one inch from both walls. Nobody but nobody was allowed to touch them. Other staff may place their tannin-stained mugs in descending order of seniority along the right-hand side.

I've just had a thought; maybe we could appoint Ken as mentor to young Bates.

Back on the verandah I spotted Spud Murphy, the school bully, and his three hangers on, pushing the new boy, Michael Booth up against the fence.

"Murphy," I called out. "You and your friends. Get yourselves over to those rubbish bins in the corner and pick up all that rubbish in the playground. Hurry up. Get to it. Now."

Murphy and his mates shuffled off mumbling among themselves. I looked up to see Spike McTavish pushing his bike.

"Hello Spike, good to see you back with us for another year. I've missed your smiling face. Did you have a good holiday? I see you've already met up with our new boy, Michael. I'm going to appoint you as his very special friend and guardian. I want you to show him around the school and look after him. If anything happens, mind you, I'm going to hold you personally responsible. Do you understand me?"

"Yes Sir," replied Spike, shoulders forward, eyes down, feet shuffling back and forth while turning the bike handles side to side.

"You're a good boy, Spike. Don't let me down. Now be off with you and tell those other friends of yours to hurry up with that rubbish"

Out the front of the school there was a large group of parents and pupils chatting away, catching up on the last six weeks. Oh, my goodness, there is Mrs Blackett, Mrs Thompson and Mrs Blewett, all coming to the gate at the same time. This could be interesting.

Janice Blackett lost her husband in the New Guinea campaign but is now living with Ken Thompson. Merle Thompson, his wife, is living with Peter Blewett, and Peter's wife Shirley, has

160

invited Butch Edwards to move in after Butch's wife left to go north at Christmas time with a travelling small goods salesman. So, what's surprising about that? In Gubba Creek, a change is as good as a holiday, and everyone seems happy.

There they were all together at the gate chatting like old friends and although the kids are with different fathers, they still get on very well. Thank goodness. That will make life easier at school. Seeing them has jogged my memory about the golden rule in country towns; don't talk about someone's spouse because you can't be certain who belongs to whom at any particular time, who's paying the rent, how long that will last and who will be next? It's the old musical beds game.

Emerging from the office at the other end of the verandah emerged Mr Creighton-Brown, the new Principal, trying sternly to look like a man in control. He was accompanied by the most gorgeous, tall, slender, willowy blonde with legs right up to her arm pits. She moved with the grace and style of Rita Hayworth. She must be the replacement for Mrs Morrison who retired last year. Creighton-Brown stomped past us on his way to the women's staff room without so much as a "Hello" or "I'd like you to meet Miss So and So."

I've taken an instant dislike to that man. In hindsight, old skinflint Fogarty, with all his faults last year, might not have been that bad after all.

I took a look at Andrew whose attention was riveted on the new woman. He was already thinking how he could invite her to go home with him that afternoon. I could just see it now; Rita

Hayworth and The Lone Ranger riding off into the sunset on that old rusty Malvern Star bike of his. Hi Ho Silver. Up, up and away.

"Never mind Andy," I said to him. "I've got the answer to your bachelor prayers. I heard Laura Briggs is after a good husband and she's got her eye on you."

Andy was not amused.

I've had a better thought. Why couldn't I offer my services to show the new woman the sights of town in my old Austin car this afternoon? I'd have to get in quick before the sons of all the rich graziers with their big Chevies, broad brimmed hats and fat wool cheques got a sniff that there was a new bird in town.

I could take her down for a quiet drink in the saloon bar at the Commercial pub, and then drive around to the river park near the billabong to watch the wild ducks and then go up to Billy Goat hill to see the sun set over the western plains. Getting better with every thought, but I wondered if those long legs of hers would fit into the Austin?

I might just wander down to the women's staff room to say hello to the women from last year and they might just happen to introduce me to the new members of staff while I'm there.

As I walked past the men's staff room the door burst open and Tommy Hobbs, the English/Drama teacher, dashed for the safety of the verandah followed by a hail of books, chalk and dusters. Tommy must have been stirring them up in there. Thank goodness for the Tommy Hobbs in this world. He was the real character on staff. Life was never dull in the staff room with him there.

This could be a good year. But then the flaming bell blasted through my ear drums calling all the faithful to the early morning assembly. Damn it. I won't have time to go the women's staff room.

"Righto you lot. Off arses and on classes," shouted Bazza Welsh from the staff room as he pushed young Anderson towards the door.

"Bazza," retorted Ken Smythe "This is a school and we do have standards. Try to get your mind above the lavatory can for once and set an example for the others."

Creighton-Brown stood to attention in front of the assembly, hand in a frozen salute to shade his eyes from the searing sun. He scanned the assembled mob with the sharpness of a wedge tailed eagle. "We will start with the Lord's Prayer and God Save the King."

"Rusty. Stop picking your nose," I said. "Stand up straight and pay attention to the principal while he's talking to you. Mary, stop kicking dust onto Alison's shoes."

As the Principal presented his boring sermon about good behaviour and expected standards, I looked over the new recruits. Could they be a brighter lot this year? More talented? Better sports? Better behaved? Would they have helpful uncomplaining parents? I doubt it. That boy, third from the end, is poking his finger into the ear of the boy in front. I'll have to watch him.

The little girl in the middle was crying. It was her first day ever in a school. She came from a station from out past the mulga. But let's look on the positive side. Most of last years' football and cricket team were still here so we should thrash the other schools this year. Mary Hughes was back. She should be dux, and her mum was the best helper at the fete and at sporting carnivals.

Overall, it was a mixed bag; socks up, socks down, no socks, no shoes, shirts clean, shirts dirty, hair done or untidy, washed or stinky. We've got them all at our select academy here at the District School. The incoming tide brought in some top-quality fish but, oh my goodness, there's some flotsam washed up there on the shore as well. Well, here's my first class this year. Let's go.

"Come now boys and girls, pay attention. Left turn. Come on, all you Bradmans and Einsteins, Melbas and Messengers, Dickens and Shakespeares, pick up your bags and follow me to Room 8. Come on, smarten up, show them that this is the best class in the school. Jump to it."

Like little nuggets of gold, those kids were rough on the outside but rich through and through. This will be a good year. Let's go.

Roger the Lodger

"Gawd strewth Vera, the baby looks like a bloody skinned rabbit with myxomatosis. Ya sure ya picked up the right kid from the hospital? He don't look like mine."

With that simple expression John Michael Peters was welcomed into the world by his father, and from that day on he was always known as 'Rabbit' Peters. He grew into a scrawny, weedy kid with rounded shoulders, arched back and skinny bow legs, more suited to sitting on a horse than walking or running.

That seemed appropriate because Rabbit's father was a drover and had him on a horse before he could walk. He put young Rabbit up on the back of One-Eyed Barney, a quiet broken-down hack, and led him around the paddock until the boy could take control of the reins himself. To help himself stand on his own two feet, Rabbit would hang onto Barney's bridle for support with his other arm around the neck of Blackie, the old Border Collie-Kelpie cross. His parents never worried when he was with those two.

Rabbit wanted to follow in his father's footsteps and become a drover. He had a special feeling for horses, dogs and sheep and they all responded to his quiet firm commands. He spent hours talking to the animals, preferring them to people. He could be seen any afternoon down in the back paddock, whistling to the dogs until they followed his commands to round up any sheep, pigs and chooks unfortunate enough to be grazing on the sparse vegetation within his span of vision. On one such afternoon he was even seen directing the dogs to turn a red bellied black snake back to the bend in the river at the back of their property.

Rabbit was often the butt of jokes in the playground at school. He was small and had a quiet manner, making him a perfect target for the bullies. They would flip off his hat and trip him in the dust and claim it was an accident before laughing at his expense. One day they threatened to put his head down the dunny can. They took off his trousers and threw them out into the playground. Rabbit's dash to retrieve his pants was met by whistles and laughter from both the boys and girls playing games outside the toilet block. The next day Rabbit decided to take a stand.

"Come here, ya skinny little runt," shouted Butch Walters, the school bully. "I'm gunna belt the livin' daylights outa you. It won't take much. Look at ya. Ya ain't got enough muscle to knock over a fly. To be fair I'll keep one hand behind me back."

Five of Butch's mates burst out laughing at poor little Rabbit facing the dreaded school bully.

Butch turned to his mates. "Hey, take a look at this hunk of sheep dung. What'll we do with him?"

Rabbit was standing near the horse stalls in the corner of the playground. He slowly hitched up his trousers, picked up a bridle from the post and walked slowly towards his tormentor. In one swift movement he lashed the leather bridle across Butch's face. As Butch lurched forward to grab him, Rabbit swung the bridle back across the other side of Mick's face opening up a deep cut below his ear. The dry air crackled with static electricity. For a minute nobody said a word. Even the birds were frightened to speak and the leaves on the trees hung dead still in anticipation of an impending thunderstorm.

"Look what ya did to Butch, ya mongrel," shouted Bluey. "Why don't ya say somethin?"

Rabbit, with a confident determination that showed he meant business, picked up the bridle again and walked slowly in the direction of Bluey, picking up a whip on the way. He said nothing. He preferred actions rather than wasting time clapping his lips on words.

Bluey and the other boys stepped back, keeping a safe distance between themselves and the silent assassin.

Rabbit stopped, spread his legs and stared at the retreating group; his arms spread to swing the bridle or whip if required.

"Now listen up you lot. Nobody takes my trousers. Do ya git it? Now piss orf you lot; git lost; or I'll put this whip around ya legs."

The stunned group retreated, and from that moment Rabbit was treated with the respect he deserved.

From that day on, nobody annoyed Rabbit again and his friends took comfort at being seen with him, enjoying his quiet company and protection.

When Rabbit was eleven, his father took him from school to go droving with the team.

"Bloody useless ya being at school," said his father. "They ain't learning ya nothing there. Ya better orf comin' with me on the road and doin' a decent day's work."

Rabbit was in seventh heaven and never set foot back in that school again. He and his horse moved as one and with his dogs he could drove large numbers of cattle or sheep, grazing easily on both sides of the road or in the long paddock for months at a time.

When his parents died, Rabbit took over the team and he was soon sought after by graziers who wanted their stock treated with care. At the end of each drive, he would return to his parent's shack. It was at the two-mile bend on the creek, next door to Tony and Maria, the Italian vegetable farmers. They would always give him vegetables and he would kill a hogget and respond in kind.

One day, while having a beer at the Railway Hotel, Rabbit was introduced to Rosie, a quiet, softly spoken girl who had come from Boggabilla to get away from her parents. She had a job helping Mrs Reilly in the kitchen at the pub. When Rabbit found she had nowhere to stay he offered her a room in the shack on condition she looked after the house while he was away droving. She was quietly shy with a quirky sense of humour, but had a fiercely independent streak that won the respect of Rabbit because he knew that she could look after herself while he was away.

This arrangement worked well and he was happy with the tidiness of the shack when he returned home. After one of his long trips home, Rosie asked him to show her how to light the chip heater to get some hot water for the bath.

"It's Wensdee night and I like to have a bath on Wensdee," explained Rosie.

Rabbit explained the process to Rosie and watched everything she did while moving closer to not miss a thing.

"You just cut this kindling nice and small and put it here on the lit paper in the heater."

In no time the heater was going whoomp, whoomp, whoomp, whoomp as the hot water gushed into the bath.

Rosie stood up and got undressed. "By the time I git finished," she said, "the water will be cold. So why don't you jump in too, so we both gits the hot water? I won't look at ya. Promise."

Well, would you believe it? Whoomp, whoomp, whoomp, whoomp... there was quite a head of steam built up that night and one thing led to another, and nine months later, young 'Bunny' Peters, a dead set ringer of his father, came into the world.

Over the next few years, the Wensdee night ritual was played out again and again. Young Bunny was followed by the next baby called Squint, because of her sideways, half-closed look at everything as if the sun was so bright. She could not stand the glare. Then along came Bubbles who spent most of her time happily talking and singing to her one-eyed Teddy. The fourth child to arrive at the two mile was named Michael, but became known as Re, as in Re Peters, because he suffered from a bad stutter.

"Bloody hell Rosa, why ya get prego again?" asked Tony Morelli. "You tell me you no want more kidsa."

"Ah Tony, I know what I tell ya. But it's always Wensdee nights, I can't help it," answered Rosie.

"Whats this Wensdee nighta? Whats you talkin' about?"

"Well Rabbit and me always have a hot bath on Wensdee nights. Ya know, Tony," said Rosie, "I don't have ta tell ya what

169

happens next do I? It jist happens. It's because it's Wensdee night. Da ya git what I mean? 'Av I got ta write it down for ya eh?"

For the next few years family life at the two-mile settled down to a routine. That was until, at the Railway Hotel one afternoon, Rabbit met Roger O'Sullivan, who had moved from Queensland to get a job at the local sale yards. Roger had a nervous twitch of his head and shoulders, and had difficulty keeping eye contact with the person opposite. But after a few beers he and Rabbit strung a few words together in what loosely could be called a conversation with 'yep', 'sure thing', 'great', 'blood oath' and 'mate' scoring highly in the word count.

Rabbit offered him a bed at the end of the verandah with the kids, providing he chopped the wood, cleaned the yard and did any chores for Rosie while Rabbit was away droving. This arrangement worked well for the next two years and everyone was happy.

But, after a very long drive of four months, Rabbit returned to find Rosie at the door to greet him with an odd stunned mullet look on her face.

"What's the matter Rosie? Aren't ya pleased ta see me?" asked Rabbit.

"Of course, I'm pleased ta see ya Rabbit. I've been bustin me gut waitin for ya to come home to give ya me good news."

"What bloody news? Are the kids okay? What's happened?" asked Rabbit.

"Na. The kids is okay. Stop worrying. I want to tell ya that Roger and me are goin' ta git married"

Rabbit took hold of his hat, shifted it up and down and then flicked his head from side to side as if to dislodge an imaginary beetle from his left ear. He looked down at his dusty boots and the hole where his right toe was starting to poke through. Stretching his back to the left, he eased the pressure on his right hip where he had landed off a wild brumby he had tried to break in the previous week. Then he looked Rosie directly in the eye again.

"If ya wanted ta git married why didn't ya marry me?" he asked.

"Because ya never bloody well asked me, did ya?" said Rosie. "But Rabbit, I want ya to be happy for me and I want you to do something very special for me. Will ya give me away at the wedding?"

Rabbit turned slowly and went out the door without a word. He walked with his dogs beside him, scratching his pants, as if trying to shake loose some Bathurst burs in the lining. Over the fence and down to the bend in the creek he went. Gone two hours and Rosie got worried.

The dogs came back first, thankful for the opportunity to have a drink and lie down in the shade. Rabbit shuffled in, head down, hands moving in and out of his pockets in a nervous attempt to dry the perspiration. Stopping inside the door, Rabbit looked Rosie in the eye for at least a minute before speaking.

"I will give ya away, but there's one condition," drawled Rabbit to an expectant Rosie. "There's no bloody way I'm gunna light that bloody chip heater for you and Roger. Do ya git what I mean?"

Rosie was all over him, kissing and hugging until he pushed her away with embarrassment. "You have made me so happy, thank you, thank you so much. I must rush off to tell Roger."

The Methodist minister wouldn't conduct the ceremony because they had never been to his church, but the newly appointed Anglican minister, the Reverend West, had no such qualms, providing he could christen the children at the same time. He reckoned that one wedding and four christenings in one week looked pretty good on God's register.

On the chosen day, Squint and Bubbles ran excitedly down to the back paddock to pick some purple Patterson's Curse, yellow 'wet-the-bed' daisies and some red geraniums from the back fence and tied them into little bouquets with binder twine for the bridal party. Everyone got washed up at the tank stand, put on clean clothes and did their hair, some for the first time in a month.

When everyone was ready, the bridal party set off in formal order down the dirt track for the two miles walk to town... Rabbit and Rosie in front, then Maria, the Matron of Honour, Squint and Bubbles, the bridesmaids, Bunny and Re, the groomsmen, Roger the groom and then Tony, the best man, bringing up the rear. Along the way neighbours emerged from their houses to clap and cheer the wedding party and Rabbit felt proud to be recognized as the leader of the group and to be there to support Rosie.

After the ceremony they all retired to the saloon bar of the Railway Hotel where Mrs Reilly organized some of the local CWA women to put on a spread and Dan put on a free keg of beer to get the married couple off to a good start. When they got home Roger moved into the bedroom and Rabbit parked himself on the verandah bed. Other than that, nothing much changed at the two-mile bend. And that's the way it was for the next couple of years.

However, when Rabbit came home from a very long drive to Victoria, he found Rosie in tears.

"Whatsa matter? What's 'appened to the kids? Stop snifflin'. Tell me what's wrong."

Rosie handed him a piece of paper. "Look at this note. It was on me bed yesterdee when I came home from helping Mrs Reilly at the pub. What ya make of it?"

Rabbit grabbed the note. The message was clear.

"GAWN BACK TO NORTH QUEENSLAND.
SORRY. ROGER"

"The bloody mongrel, he's gawn and left ya. I always thought he had some of that mongrel Kelpie cross in 'im. They bred too much of the dingo into that strain. Can't trust 'em. Good while you keep 'em under control, but take ya bloody eye off 'em and they piss orf looking for a better feed elsewhere. Ya better orf without 'im love. He's not worth a pinch of lizard shit. You'll never see 'im agin. An' if he comes sniffin' around here, I'll give 'im a touch of lead poisoning behind the left ear, just to give 'im somethin' ta think about and hurry 'im on his way back ta Queensland. The rotten bastard, doin' that to you. He didn't have the guts to tell you straight to your face. Always had that shifty look about him. Castratin' 'im with a rusty knife would be too good for blokes like that."

That was probably the longest unbroken speech Rabbit had ever made in his life but it showed his feelings for Rosie and for the hurt she felt. After a moment's silence he had a bright idea.

173

"Hey Rosie, now that Roger's gone, why don't you and me git married? I'm askin' you this time."

"Ya can't do that Rabbit. I'm already married. It's not right. I asked the Revend West and he said it was bigmy or something like that. He said it's agin the law and we could be locked up if we did it. Ya don't want that, do ya?"

There was another long pause of silence while he tried to absorb the impact of her rejection. "Hey Rosie, what day is it?"

"I ain't thought about that," replied an irritated Rosie. "I've been too busy worryin' about Roger's note to be thinkin' about what day it is...Hey! Wait a minute! It's Wensdee! It's Wensdee night, Rabbit. Go git some kindlin'. We's gunna have ourselves a bath. There's nothing agin the law for havin a bath on a Wensdee night is there?"

Rabbit filled an extra-large box with kindling, and got the heater roaring. WHOOMP, WHOOMP, WHOOMP, WHOOMP, WHOOMP. The walls of the bathroom vibrated to the rhythm of the heater as Rosie and Rabbit slipped into the hot water. WHOOMP, WHOOMP, WHOOMP, WHOOMP.

"Tonight, Rabbit, I'm gunna look at you, I promise," said Rosie with a grin.

Tony and Maria next door walked out onto their verandah. "Bloody hell Maria," said Tony. "It must be Wensdee night. That bathroom chimney next door is pushin out lotsa smoke and steam tonight."

WHOOMP, WHOOMP, WHOOMP, WHOOMP.

Life at the two-mile bend was back to normal.

WHOOMP, WHOOMP, WHOOMP, WHOOMP.

174

What Am I Worth?

"Hey Lofty," said Shorty, "How would ya like a few days' work down at the yards. Old Hughie McIntosh, the Stock and Station agent, wants us to do a few weeks dippin' sheep, doin' some weedin', fixin' fences, yardin' at the sales day and loadin' the sheep inta the railway trucks after the sales. What ya think, eh?"

Kevin, otherwise known as Lofty Case, because he could just raise himself to five feet two on tippy toes, thought about the proposal for a minute and asked; "What about Gravel Rhodes? Can Hughie put the three of us on for that time?"

"Yeah, I asked Hughie and he agreed, so Gravel can do it while he's on holidays from school."

So the three mates; Shorty Long, a six foot three raw boned eighteen year old, Gravel Rhodes, a scruffy layabout, mostly too tired to get out of his own way, and Lofty Case, a wiry little devil, all turned up at the yards off Jindalong Road at seven o'clock the next morning to start work.

Hughie McIntosh, broad brimmed hat, neat blue shirt with glasses case and pens in top pocket, moleskin trousers and riding boots, hands on hips, met them at the auctioneer's pen, impatient to get on with the day's work.

"The first thing I want you to do," he said, "is to go down the road this side of the dump and help Ding Dong bring up those three hundred sheep he's getting out of the holding paddock. Get them into that paddock over there and put them all through the dip. After that I want you to start yarding each truckload of sheep as the farmers bring in. Here's the sheet to tell you which pen each lot goes into. And if they get mixed up, I'll have your balls for breakfast. Ding Dong and the dogs will help you with the yarding. Now get to it and come and tell me when you've got it done."

"How much will we git paid fer that, Mr McIntosh?" asked Gravel.

"Fifteen shillings a day and an extra five bob for loading the sheep into the railway trucks. We start loading the sheep into the railway trucks at two o'clock in the morning. Now get to it or you'll get nothing."

They trooped down the road past the cemetery towards the dump where they met Harry Bell, known locally as Ding Dong, who was getting ready to bring the flock onto the road. They explained they'd been sent by Hughie McIntosh to help him with the sheep, but they got barely an audible grunt for a response. Ding Dong was not into communicating with humans unless he had to. He put his dogs on a higher plateau than people because dogs never argued, always did as they were told, came when he called, worked all day without complaint, greeted him with a smile and a tail wag and they didn't expect to be paid at the end of the day. He and his dogs Rusty, Spot, Blacky and Bitzer were a great team.

Shorty Long and his two mates came in behind the sheep and started to help move them out onto the road towards the sale yards. Ding Dong climbed back into his battered Bedford ute and gave instructions and a series of ear-splitting whistles to the four dogs who did all the hard work for him. The three boys tried to work out what this bloke was all about and they had a good laugh about his appearance.

A picture of sartorial elegance, Ding Dong wore a beanie that looked like an old tea cosy. A tattered cardigan loosely covered a flannel undershirt that looked as though it had never been off his back and was stained with dark dribbles of tea and food. It was stiff with sweat and dust and moulded to his chest. The torn trousers covering his bowed legs were held up with binder twine. His boots were re-soled with rubber cut from an old car tyre. The front of one boot was held together with a twist of fencing wire. He was permanently surrounded by a highly charged cloud of stale body odour, flies and the smoke that curled upwards from the cigarette always dangling from his bottom lip.

The lads and Ding Dong worked all morning dipping the sheep and moving them to the holding paddock. After smoko they yarded the truck loads coming in from the farms ready for the Friday sales. They were good workers and ran back and forth to make sure that the sheep went into the right pens and there was no mixing of the flocks. Gravel Rhodes kept the record sheets up to date, writing down the name of each farm and the number of sheep in each pen, double checking with the others to make sure of their accuracy. He might have looked half asleep most of the time but he had a good brain for figures and organisation.

"Hey, Shorty, get a look at old Ding Dong over there. He jist sits on the fence and shouts or whistles at the dogs all day. He hasn't moved his arse all day. We're doin' all the work while he sits on his bum," said Lofty to his mate.

"Why should we be doin' all the work?" chimed in Gravel Rhodes "You'd think he'd get in and push a few sheep around to make it look as if he's workin'. Why the hell would Hughie put him on in the first place? I thought Hughie was smarter than that."

"Go over there and tell him to get in and help us or we'll give him a kick up the you know what," demanded Shorty.

"You go an' tell im' yerself mate. I don't want to go anywhere near 'im. He stinks. I'd rather give his dogs a hug. At least they're doin' a good day's work."

"Hey, Ding Dong," shouted Shorty. "How about getting off ya arse and come over here an' help us with these sheep. Get up the front and get the leaders through that gate so we can get the rest of them into that pen."

"Up Rusty," called Ding Dong. "Way back Blacky. Sit Spot. Come Bitzer. Good dogs."

With a combination of short commands and whistles the dogs had the sheep through the gate and all yarded. Ding Dong never gave a response or even a sign of recognition that the others were even within cooee of him, and he had not moved one inch from his position on the railing in the corner of the pen.

"I wonder how much Hughie pays the old bastard 'cause he wouldn't work in an iron lung even if all of us were there pushing the air into him with a big set of bellows at both ends," said Lofty

"Hey, Ding Dong," shouted Shorty. "How much does old Hughie pay you for proppin' up that fence all day? I reckon it'd be a pretty important job to make sure that the posts don't fall down while the sheep are in the yard. It must take a lot of effort to hold 'em up, eh?"

There was no immediate response. Ding Dong took some time to call in the dogs, give them a pat and half a biscuit each before pouring water into his pannikin for each to have a drink. When that was finished, he turned slowly towards Shorty. "Well sonny boy, it's like this. Hughie pays me thirty shillings a day and gives me five bob for each of my dorgs. Now if you three'll only stop talkin' and stop scarin' the sheep we might be able to git orn with it and finish the job before Christmas."

"I'm gunna go 'n have a talk with Hughie," snorted Shorty stalking off in a huff.

Hughie McIntosh was over by the shed giving instructions to his secretary Vera, when he was interrupted by Shorty.

"Hey Hughie, is it right that you're payin' ol' Ding Dong twice as much as us and you even pay him for his dogs as well. Bloody hell, the four dogs get more than me and they're only dogs. Is that what you bloody well think I'm worth? Is it eh? Is that what you reckon? Is that what you think of us? We've been working our guts out all day and he's been sittin' on the bloody fence doin' stuff all. He hasn't raised a bloody finger all day, hasn't worked up a sweat, hasn't moved a muscle. He just sits and whistles and shouts at the dogs. You treat us like dog shit and think that's all we're worth. What've ya got ta say about that now?"

Hughie was annoyed by this intrusion but kept control by taking his time talking to Vera before slowly turning to face the callow youth.

"Well, Shorty me boy, you want to know what you're worth? Then let me ask you some simple questions. How fast can you run the hundred yards?"

"Twelve seconds at the carnival last week. That's pretty good, ain't it?"

"Not bad," replied Hughie, pausing to watch another truck coming up the road, "for a young bloke like you, but let me tell you that Ding Dong's dog Rusty can run that distance in one third of that time. Now, how many meals do you have a day?"

"Three; breakfast, lunch and dinner," replied Shorty, feeling pleased with himself.

"Well," said Hughie. "Add two smokos and a bag of chips and a milk shake at Joe's café on the way home and that means that you eat ten times what Rusty eats. Now, how many sheep could you take from this paddock to the one across the road by yourself?"

"I reckon I could get twenty across there, no hassle."

"Well, Rusty could take twenty times twenty across the road and keep them calm all the way. So, let me see now," said Hughie, looking skywards as he did his mental calculations. "If I do my sums right, that makes you one third of one tenth of one twentieth of bugger all. That's what you're worth compared to Rusty the dog."

Shorty, somewhat stunned by the answer, took two steps back as he was in two minds, whether to continue to argue or retreat gracefully.

"Now on top of what I pay Rusty," Hughie continued, "I also pay Ding Dong for his good looks and his intelligence and some more for the other three dogs, and they're all better than Rusty. I think that's a pretty fair estimate of what you're worth, don't you think?"

Shorty started to retreat to the safety of the sheep pens with his mates but was stopped by Hughie's further assessment.

"And now that you've wasted twenty minutes of my time and yours, I'm going to dock your wages by five shillings and if you haven't got all those truck loads done in the next hour, I'll give you nothing for the day. We've got a sale tomorrow and I can't waste my time arguing with you. So, what do you think of that?"

"Jeez, Hughie that's a bit rough don't ya think?"

"Well, being the gentleman that I am, I'll tell you what I'll do for you, Shorty. Because I like you so much, I'll give you a very special award for the day. It's called a DCM."

Shorty lifted his head and shoulders, looking both pleased with himself but also apprehensive.

"What's the DCM, Hughie?" he asked

"Don't Come Monday."

Cheers

It was a hot, languid, breathless day in Gubba Creek. It was the week before Christmas, but there was very little to celebrate because of the prolonged drought. Only two people could be seen along Main Street, and they were showing little sign of life. They found it difficult to move one foot after the other. A stray dog lay panting under the pepper tree at the corner.

In the public bar of the Commercial pub a few drinkers sat on stools, head and shoulders slumped over their beers. The drinks quickly warmed in the short distance from the bar top to their mouths. Puddin', the barman, kept wiping the same glass, waiting patiently for another customer to relieve the boredom. Then through the door burst Squeaky Atkins, the barman from the Railway pub. He was Puddin's great mate.

"Now listen to me, Puddin'," shouted Squeaky. "I've come over here to pick up our keg of beer that they loaded by mistake onto your truck this morning at the railway."

"What the bloody hell are ya on about, Squeaky? We haven't got ya bloody keg, mate. We just picked up our lot from the railway shed this morning. Your lot wus on the other side of the shed. Here, do ya wanna a proper beer, mate? It's on the house for me old mate," replied Puddin' with a smile.

Let's look at these two odd characters. On our left we had Squeaky Atkins, barman at the Railway Hotel…five foot two inches in his elevated shoes, seven stone two ounces dripping wet. He was a former jockey, with a rapid fire, high pitched, nasal twang. His prominent nose was covered by a forward thrusting cloth cap. He often acted as a go between for the customers of Holy Moses, the local SP bookmaker. He wrote down the bets on the inside of an old cigarette packet he kept in his back pocket.

On our right we had Puddin' Starkey, eighteen stone, floral faced, with a frontal overhang so large he'd have to pay a boy a penny to check if his fly was undone because he couldn't see it for himself. His shirt was so tight that the middle buttons had difficulty holding onto the holes on the other side. The gaps exposed a sweaty, hairy navel for all to see.

Puddin' was a big friendly bear of a man, good at keeping the customers happy but he was a little too inclined to match them drink for drink.

"Don't 'me-ole-mate' me, Puddin'," screamed Squeaky, moving quickly from side to side to get a better look at Puddin' between the drinkers at the bar. "You're a thievin' bastard. Ya took your kegs for the Commercial and then nicked an extra one from the Railway Hotel lot from the other side. Let's go down to the cellar and git it. I've got Charlie out the front with the ute to help load it and take it back down the street."

"Go take a runnin' jump at yerself, Squeaky. You've been drinking too much of that cheap piss whiskey you sell down at the

Railway. It'll rot ya guts and brain, mate. Your trouble mate is that ya can't even count the fingers on one hand let alone ten kegs of beer. Here mate, have a schooner on the house. At least we clean the pipes here and we don't git the cockroaches and slime like at your dump."

"I just want me keg of beer, not the slops from the drip tray ya serve these poor bastards here. It's flat, warm and stale. It's been lying in that tray there behind the bar since last week. Ya might as well give 'em 'orse piss, Puddin'."

Squeaky pushed Twilight Black to one side to get closer to the bar. "At least at the Railway the beer's fresh."

Puddin' swished the tea towel over his shoulder, slammed down the glass and slapped his other hand onto the bar. "Listen Squeaky, I'm trying ta be nice ta ya cause you're me old mate, even if ya do work in that brothel at the other end of town. But ya startin' ta piss me orf and I'm losin' me patience real quick. So, take yerself and Charlie back ta the railway shed and try countin' ya kegs agin. This time use ya fingers on both hands."

"Listen ta me, ya robbin' bastard," snorted Squeaky. "If ya don't go down and git me keg I'm gunna come round there and take ya apart."

"Jeez, Squeaky, ya musta been on that metho and boot polish agin, have ya? What bloody army have ya got to help ya this time?" Puddin' stepped back with a confident smile.

"I don't need any army, ya big fat Puddin' prick. I'll take ya apart right now meself. Come on, put up yer dooks."

Puddin's beer belly bounced with increasing mirth. "Squeaky, in a fair fight between you and a butterfly with its wings tied back, I'd still put me money on the butterfly."

Squeaky jumped as high as he could and grabbed Puddin' by the shirt front and started swinging with his other hand, to no effect because, at full stretch, he could still only reach Puddin's shirt pocket.

On any other day Puddin' and Squeaky were the best of mates; the unlikely couple; the Abbott and Costello of Gubba Creek; even though they worked for rival hotels. Whenever the Flying Squad was expected in town it was those two who organised a cricket match between the pubs at the Six Mile so that when the police arrived there was nobody left in town. They tried to organise their days off to coincide with the picnic races at Bomgarra, Karingee or Jindalong.

Squeaky always talked to his former jockey mates to get the good oil and to find out in which race the favourite was to be pulled. Together they ran the local football club where Puddin' was the president and Squeaky was the secretary and treasurer, with both their hotels sponsoring the local team.

But today was not what you would call normal in the hotel business in Gubba Creek. It had been a very long, hot, stinking summer; the fourth year of an extremely bad drought. Everyone was busy trying to get the wheat harvest in before the locust plague ate the crops to ground level. To add insult to injury, the brewery workers and train drivers had gone on strike in the city. That meant beer was in short supply, and what was available arrived late or not at all. In that superheated atmosphere, even the best of friends, were at each other's throats.

For Puddin' to be accused by his mate Squeaky of stealing a keg of beer on a day like this was the last straw.

Now let's get back to the Commercial Hotel bar where Squeaky, the Pomeranian pup, was desperately clinging to the shirt front of Puddin', the Great Dane, who was trying to shake off his aggressor. Twilight Black looked up from his beer to see Sergeant Jim Morris walk past the window. He called him in to settle the dispute.

"Twilight, get behind the bar and look after the customers until these two sort out their differences," commanded Jim.

He eyed the combatants, grabbed them by the ears and said, "Now you two, get out to the back yard and don't come back here until you kiss and make up. Now get to it or I'll be forced to take you down to the station."

"Aren't ya gunna stop 'em, Sarge?" whispered Rowdy.

"No. Let them sort it out. They won't cause any damage. Squeaky can't reach Puddin's armpit and Puddin' is so slow that any punch he throws will take a week to get there. They'll sort it out. Just have a schooner of beer waiting for them when they come back in."

When the two finally had pushed and shoved each other to exhaustion, Squeaky limped off shouting revenge in a higher pitch than usual. But on his way through the back bar, he noticed Harry Withers, a handyman who did some work for both hotels.

"Hey Harry," he whispered in a tone not audible to the others. "Do me a favour will ya? When ya go down the cellar here this arvo to check the pipes, slip the bolt on the underside of the cellar door will ya, mate? There's a quid on the winner of the last race this Satdee fer ya mate if ya do that for me. Thanks mate. I promise, I'll look after ya."

At midnight Squeaky and Charlie parked the ute on the Great Northern Road outside the Commercial. They lifted the cellar door, crawled down the ramp and rolled a keg back up top. Nobody in town was awake to witness this little escapade.

Puddin' had gone home that night believing that Squeaky would get over his aggro. The heat must have caused a simple error in his counting. Puddin' was determined to make it up to him by promising to drive him to the New Year races at Bomgarra where they could enjoy a fun day away from the pubs. But the next morning he was furious when he discovered one keg was missing and the latch on the cellar door was ajar.

Shop keepers sweeping the footpath outside their establishments in the main street were shocked when Puddin' did not respond to their greetings in his usual jocular manner. He puffed, snorted and swore. The veins on his crimson face stood out like red sand dunes in the desert. He swore all the way to the Railway Hotel.

"Ya stinkin' little slimy rat and I thought you was me mate," shouted Puddin' in a voice that could be heard the length of the main street.

"Listen ta me ya big fat lump of lard," Squeaky replied. "That was our keg of beer and my drinkers deserve to have their share in the best pub in town. Now piss orf 'cause ya lowerin' the tone at this end of town."

For ten minutes the two pushed and grunted through the saloon bar, past the toilets and kitchen and into the back yard, with others looking on in amusement.

When they were about to collapse, Charlie came through the back door, took them by the shirt fronts and pulled them apart.

"Now back off you two or I'll drop the both of you where you stand. Don't even think of complaining or I'll put me fist down ya throat and I'll pull ya guts back up through ya mouth."

The two were stunned by Charlie's intervention.

He continued. "Now listen to me. Somethin's come up and we need to sit down an' have a chat to see what we're gunna do about it. So, let's go back into the bar and have a beer to cool off."

Charlie wanted both of them to calm down and be clear in their thinking before he told them the news.

Puddin' and Squeaky stood back, leaned against the tank stand, took some deep breaths and calmed down.

Charlie poked them in the chest. "For a start, before we go inside, turn on that tap and wash your faces and have a drink. Cool down. You two look bloody awful."

After they had calmed down, Charlie led them into the saloon bar, ordered a schooner each and waited until they had finished it before continuing.

"Now listen carefully. I've just found out that the goods train that's carrying our Christmas supply of beer has been delayed by the strike an' won't be here 'til Saturdee."

"No problem, mate," said Squeaky "we can pick up our supply from the railway shed on Saturdee, can't we? What's the problem?"

"But that new Station Master, that bastard Atkinson, he's the problem. He's an Elder of the Church and President of the Temperance Society, and he's the most miserable skinflint wowser this side of Timbuktu. He can't stand alcohol or anyone who drinks it. He says it is a mortal sin to drink and we'll all go to hell and face fire, brimstone and damnation if we do."

"Stuff him," said Puddin'. "We'll just go an' git the kegs and he can go and take a running jump at 'imself."

"Ya missin' the point," said Charlie. "He's decided that he won't open the sheds on Saturdee because it's a holiday weekend. Because there's no more trains 'til after New Year, the railway office will be closed. So, there'll be no more supplies for over a week and no railway staff will be allowed to open up for us."

Puddin' and Squeaky stormed out of the bar, like a Disney version of the ant and the elephant on the warpath. They stomped along the Great Northern Road, across Railway Parade to the station. They confronted the implacable Mr Atkinson. He was as stubborn and immovable as a piece of highland granite as he listened to their pleas, threats, stamping and cussing.

"My apologies gentlemen," he said. "But you will have to accept the will of a higher Power than us mere mortals. It is God's will and there is no way I would question that. You must know He moves in mysterious ways and I believe He is showing the sinners of Gubba Creek the errors of their ways and giving them the opportunity to see the light and the goodness of the Lord. These beer strikes just didn't happen. They were ordained by God. Now, good day to you gentlemen, I have work to do."

"Aw stop beating ya lips with that crap. Save it fer ya sermon on Sundee. I bet ya love ta sip that cheap plonk they give ya at communion at church, eh? Does that make ya a sinner too?" retorted Squeaky as Mr Atkinson turned his back, strode off into his office and closed the door.

"Come on Squeaky," said Puddin'. "We can't let this happen. The town's dying of thirst, the farmers are flat out with the harvest and Christmas and New Year is a time for family celebration. Let's go and have a quiet talk with Jimmy Jackson coz I've got an idea."

They found Jimmy, who was the railway assistant, in the bar at the Railway hotel and Puddin' put forward his plan.

"Now Jimmy, you'll be at work at the railway shed on Satdee to unload the beer into the shed from the goods train but your boss Atkinson won't let us collect it 'til after New Year. This is what I want you to do. When you put the kegs in the shed, put them all on one side and then draw a diagram showing exactly where each keg is and how far away from the wall. Will ya do that fer us, Jimmy? There'll be free beer at both pubs for a month if ya do that, but don't tell anyone else."

"Sure. I can do that," said Jimmy "I can't stand that bastard, I reckon he's still got the first quid he ever earned pinned to his singlet. I'm damn sure we won't be paid any more for working on Saturday at the railway and we have to take our holidays next week with no pay to save the government money, so I'll be pleased to get one back on him."

On Saturday afternoon, Jimmy delivered the railway shed diagram clearly showing the location of all the kegs and the distances they were from the wall.

At midnight, Puddin', Squeaky and Charlie drove quietly along Railway Parade to the back of the shed which stood five feet off the ground. No lights. No talking. They made hardly a sound when they unloaded some empty kegs and rolled them under the floor of the shed. A brace and bit and a hose completed the necessary equipment for the night.

After carefully studying the diagram, Charlie was given the task of drilling a hole through the floor under the first keg but after a few minutes of quiet slow drilling he fell backwards covered in a cloud of white powder.

"Bloody hell," he exclaimed. "That Jimmy's done the wrong thing by us. I just hit a sack of flour, not a beer keg. He got it all wrong. He must be in cahoots with that bastard Atkinson. Let's go and have it out with him now."

The three musketeers stormed off across the railway tracks and down town to Jimmy's place in Crystal Street. After banging on the door and getting a mouthful of abuse from Jimmy's wife, who had been rudely awakened, they finally confronted a sleepy Jimmy standing in his pyjamas in the open doorway.

"Show me that diagram," he demanded. "Jeez, bloody hell you three, you take the prize for the biggest dumb bastards that ever walked on this earth. None of you could find your way around a brothel unless someone was hanging onto your old boy to show you where to put it. You hit the flour bags for the General Store. You stupid dickheads. Try turning the diagram around the other way

191

and you might hit pay dirt. It's quite simple. That side points north. The kegs are on the other side to the flour. Now if you can rack up half a brain between the three of you, one of you might at least understand that? Now get off with you and let me and the missus get some sleep."

Back at the railway shed Charlie drilled another hole through the floor until a gush of amber liquid spilled over him. He pushed the hose up to the keg and piped the contents into the empty keg below. When the bottom keg was filled, Squeaky pushed a bung into the hole and they loaded it onto the ute.

Each night for the next week they repeated the process filling enough kegs to last until the next night.

When the Station Master opened the shed after the New Year break, he discovered the evidence of the dirty deeds perpetrated over the Holy Week. To his way of thinking, that constituted a great sin against God and a serious breach of the law. Someone would have to pay for it. Putting on his cap and jacket he stormed off to the police station and demanded to speak to Sergeant Morris.

"I demand that you lock up those villains. They have broken into and damaged government property and stolen goods in my care. They have not only committed a serious crime but they have also sinned against the Lord as these crimes were committed during a religious holiday, the celebration of the birth of our Lord Jesus Christ. I want action now. I want those criminals locked up and the key thrown away. Show them that they can't take the law into their own hands in this town."

Big Jim Morris walked slowly around the end of the counter, scratched his ear, looked out the window, tapped the stool with his boot and moved it slowly out of the way. He leaned forward, turned his broad shoulders so that his face and right hand were directly in front of the station master's cap. He looked Mr Atkinson squarely in the eye, locking his gaze for some time before responding.

"Mr Atkinson. Let me put it this way. We are going through a very long hard drought. The heat and flies are driving everyone mad. The farmers are working their guts out to get their harvest done before the locusts eat it all. The price of wheat is low. Most parents can't afford to buy Christmas presents for the kids. The silos can't take more grain because of the rail strikes and, if the boys in town can't get some relaxation and refreshment, they are likely to commit some terrible crimes against humanity. It's my job to make certain that it does not happen in my town."

Jim paused to let that sink in before continuing. "My understanding is that the beer that was taken belonged to the hotels, and so taking it was not stealing. They only took their own supplies."

Jim looked out the window to see who was driving past and rubbed a bruise on his elbow before continuing. "I have also given that other Godly matter you raised with me some careful thought," he said, shifting his right shoulder a little closer to Atkinson's face.

"In coming to my decision, I was guided by what you have repeatedly said to me and others in this town and what you have preached in your Sunday sermons, Sir."

"What's that?" demanded the Station Master impatiently.

"Well, now that you have asked, I will tell you. You have often reminded us in your sermons that everything that happens on earth is the will of God. Isn't that so, Mr Atkinson?"

Jim paused, waiting for a response but none came.

"Well Sir," he continued, "I believe under those circumstances, the Good Lord decided to provide some well-earned relief for the people of this district. He has been the Good Shepherd to his flock. You keep telling us that He moves in mysterious ways; is that not so? I have decided therefore that it was God's will to help the good folk of Gubba Creek, wouldn't you agree?"

Jim reached back to his desk, picked up a glass and sipped the inviting cool beer.

"So cheers, Mr Atkinson."

The Italian Stallion

Sally Withers was always one of the most popular girls in the district. She was a tall, athletic, raven-haired beauty with a bubbling personality. She had a real zest for life and a positive attitude to all around her. As the only child in the family she was spoilt, but in a nice sort of way. Her parents owned a property up Coolabah Lane, off the Great Northern Road, just south of Karingee. She never tried to take advantage of her situation and was always there to help and be willing to do her share of work on the farm. Handling horses, cattle and sheep with the best of them was a breeze to her, and she willingly drove the tractor when required.

For her early education, Sally, together with kids from the neighbouring properties, attended the one teacher school at Karingee South, and the nine pupils there were like one big family. That included two special friends, Mick O'Connor and Owen Staples, both the same age and living on properties either side of the Wither's farm.

The three children were inseparable; riding horses, kicking footballs, chasing rabbits, swimming in the dam, having clod fights, shooting targets, wrestling and anything else that caught their fancy.

Their parents gave them a free hand knowing they would look after each other.

They completed their schooling at Gubba Creek District School, travelling in and out of town on the back of the old covered Bedford truck, loosely referred to as the school bus. It rattled and bounced over the twenty miles of corrugated roads morning and afternoon in dust or mud according to the season. The Karingee kids stuck together like family. Mick and Owen were zealous in keeping an eye on Sally and there were a few smart alecs who felt their wrath behind the toilet block when they tried to get fresh with her.

Sally, Mick and Owen did well at school. Their intelligence gave them a head start in the formal aspects of their education, but it was their natural sporting abilities that got much of the acclaim. Sally was the champion athlete and captained the school hockey team. She even played in the district first grade team while still at school. Mick captained the football team, played a mean cricket bat and was a good swimmer. Owen captained the cricket team, played in the football team and was a more than competent tennis player.

On finishing school, Sally got a job working for Doctor Martin as a secretary nurse while both Mick and Owen went back to work on the land. But as those three matured into young adults, the town and district gossips occupied themselves full time speculating about the special relationship that had developed between them.

They did most things together. They rode horses in the gymkhanas, went bush to shoot rabbits, caught fish, trapped foxes, travelled together to the local and district dances and went together to parties. They were there for each other to clean wounds or nurse

196

bruised egos or knees as the need demanded. They were also into community organisations such as the Show Society, sporting groups, Fire Brigade, CWA and the Red Cross.

The telephone party lines in the district ran hot with each person trying to outguess the others. Who would Sally end up with? What else was there to talk about other than the drought, fires, locusts, heat, flies and the last sheep sale? Josie, who worked the telephone exchange, could tell you that most of the conversation in the area centred on Sally's future and it went like this.

"Ya know? I think Sally should marry Mick. He's such a good-looking bloke and they can settle down on the farm and raise a bunch of kids. I'm tellin' ya; he could park his boots under my bed any time."

"Nah. It won't happen, believe me, gospel truth. I have it from the horse's mouth. Ya see; Mick's a mick, ya know. He's Catholic and Sal's a Metho. It won't work, they're not allowed to marry."

"Well, if my opinion is worth anything, I think she should marry Owen because he's Church of England and therefore he's a prod, no worries, eh?"

"She should marry Owen because he's a bit steadier. Ya know; Mick can be a bit of a tearaway, too much for the good times, not good when ya want to settle down."

"She'll go for Mick 'cause she likes a bit of the good times herself and it would never be boring with Mick. She can convert and become a mick, so it's not a problem."

Josie kept clicking into the conversations to keep abreast with the latest gossip so she could tell her Mum at the Great Northern Hotel and her close friends.

"Well, I'll put in my penny's worth. I reckon she won't marry either of them. You see, they're more like brothers and sisters and you don't marry your brother."

"What about that new teacher in town? He seems nice?"

"Come on, get a life. He's nice but he's like old Granny's custard, sweet and lukewarm. Forget about him."

"How about that young bank Johnny who came to town last month?"

"Give us a break. He's as exciting as sheep shit on sale day."

"It has to be either Mick or Owen 'cause I have it on good authority that both their parents want them to marry Sally, because she's an only child and that means that they will be able to join the properties after the parents pass on."

"She could become a nun and go off to do missionary work. It's happened before."

The threesome was oblivious to all this gossip. They were far too busy enjoying life. When the Catholic Ball came around, Sally escorted Mick. But she went with Owen to the Church of England Ball. For all other events they went as a threesome. That was until Sally decided to go to the Big Smoke for a while to stay with her Aunt Maggie and go to the Sydney Sheep Show.

Aunt Maggie talked her into staying in the city and applying for a job with a new young dentist with his surgery in her suburb. He was desperately looking for a secretary nurse. He was so smitten by Sally that he employed her straight away and over the next twelve months a close relationship developed.

Sally kept her parents informed of her feelings for her employer, but they had not taken her seriously. They were convinced she would return to Karingee and settle down with either Mick or Owen. It was now time for Sally to take her new friend for his first trip to the country.

They packed as much as they could into his small Fiat sedan and drove for eight hours to Gubba Creek, rattling over rough corrugations and pot holes for the last one hundred miles. It was so rough that the suspension broke. Sally convinced him to take the car into town and see Tom Flanagan at the garage to get it fixed. She called Tom to let him know and asked him to look after her friend and get the job done so they could get back to the city in one piece.

Main Street on this Saturday morning was quiet. It was not a sheep sale week. There were very few farmers in town and the football team and their supporters were at the Recreation Ground for the big game with Jindalong.

Ambling across the street towards the hotel, were four drovers; Tex, Butch, Dusty and Bomber. They had arrived in town that morning after bringing a herd of cattle into town from the long paddock. After a good feed at Lee's Chinese Café, they were on their way to the Commercial Pub for some liquid refreshment.

It was then that the four of them saw something quite unusual for that part of the country. Outside the garage was a young man dressed in a neatly ironed, red, white and blue striped shirt, tailored white trousers, a blue jacket and shiny black shoes you could see your face in. His dark hair was shiny and combed back in lacquered waves, and he walked with a confident swagger.

"Holy shit, Butch. Are me eyes playin' up on me? Am I seein' things or is that jist a mirage up in front of the garage up there?" asked Tex, scratching his groin with his cigarette free hand.

"Bloody hell, it couldn't be real. Let's go look at it a bit closer," replied Butch.

Buster stopped in his tracks to take a better look. "Take a look at that, Dusty. He's lit up more than the neon sign outside Joe the Greek's café."

"Hey you, come here," shouted Bomber as they approached the apparition. "Are you one of those poofters from the big smoke? Ya don't come from around here, that's fer sure."

Sally's friend turned and looked at the approaching swaggers. "I'm a friend of Sally Withers. I'm getting my car fixed at the garage."

"Don't try that crap on us mate. Sally would eat you fer breakfast. What's yer bloody name?" asked Dusty.

"My name is Roberto Sartori."

"Roberto! Roberto! What sort of a bloody name is that? You must be a bloody greasy wog boy, are ya? Why can't ya be called Bob or Jack or Jim like anyone else around here? Tell me that, wog boy."

"I was born in Italy and that name is common in my country."

"Well, you can just take yerself and all that spag back ta Italy 'cause we don't like your kind 'round here. Do ya know Tony Morelli down near the creek? He's another Spag but he's an Aussie

Spag 'cause he wus born here. Now if ya think of getting' it orf with Sally then think agin. She's a Gubba Creek girl and we look after our girls around here. Git it? Do ya?"

"I suppose ya play that sheila's game soccer, do ya? Well, ya can take ya poofter wog game with ya too," chirped in Dusty giving a backward flick of his thumb to indicate the general direction.

"Is that yer car in there wif Tom? What the bloody hell is it?" asked Buster ambling closer for a better look.

"It's a Fiat," replied Roberto.

"A fart? Did ya hear that, boys? He drives a fart. Why don't ya drive a good Aussie car like the Holden ute, eh?"

"What do ya do fer a livin'? Ya don't git yer hands dirty, that's fer sure. Sheila's hands. Look at 'em boys. Never done a decent day's work," said Bomber circling Roberto in a slow shuffle.

"I am a dentist," replied Roberto.

"Well," said Tex, drawing himself up to his full scruffy six feet in front of Roberto's compact five feet seven. "I'm gunna rearrange yer teeth, Spag 'cause I don't like 'em that way. What ya think, boys?"

Roberto stepped back as he surveyed the impending danger. "I have to warn you that I have a black belt," he cautioned.

"Ya call THAT bloody thing a belt, maate?" snorted Tex, looking at the fine piece of leather holding up Roberto's crisp white trousers. "THAT's not a belt." He pointed to his waist. "THIS is what yer call a belt."

Tex punched his thumbs over the top of his trousers, lifted his bulging stomach and thrust forward a three-inch-wide kangaroo hide strap held together by a big bronze buckle in the shape of a horseshoe on which had been welded a large bucking bronco.

"THAT belt I got fer ridin' both The Terminator and Lightnin' to a standstill at the buckjumpin' show last year. Never been done before. Now can yer see what a real belt looks like? Now come here so I can knock yer block orf."

As Tex threw the punch, Roberto dropped under the swinging arm to a defensive position. He easily deflected the blow and then stabbed his knuckles up under Tex's rib cage into his solar plexus. Tex dropped like a sack of potatoes. Had Tex been able to speak at that moment, he would have told us that Lee's chicken chow mein tasted much better going down than it did coming up.

Dusty rushed in to help his mate. He was met with a sharp kick to the knee cap before Roberto spun around and caught him across the jaw with his high arching left foot.

Bomber had fought in Jimmy Sharman's boxing tent and was considered one of the best fighters in town. Despite the evidence before him, he saw no problem in taking on someone half his size. As Bomber charged forward, Roberto kicked out his feet from under him before twisting his arm up behind his back until he cried out in pain.

Butch came to the rescue but Roberto dropped his shoulder, rolled him over his back and slammed him into the dusty pavement outside the garage door.

While all of this was happening, Mick and Owen were walking back from the Recreation Oval along Main Street on their way to the pub for a quick drink before heading home. They couldn't believe their eyes as they witnessed Roberto's demolition of the four drovers.

"Hey. You must be Sally's friend, Roberto. We've heard about you. I'm Mick and this is Owen. We're Sally's mates and we live out near her place," said Mick, making the introductions and lifting his open hands high and wide to show he was not about to attack.

"Hey calm down, mate," said Owen. "We're on your side. That was a pretty neat bit of work you did on those four clowns. Come on, we're going down to the pub for a drink. I'll let Sal know you're with us. Don't worry about the car. Tom will let us know when it's ready."

The bush telegraph was working well that day. Once Josie at the exchange heard of Roberto's exploits, the whole district knew within half an hour. By the time the three got to the pub everyone in town knew about the demolition of the drovers.

"Hey, are you the bloke who did over Tex and his mates. That was pretty neat mate. Here; have a beer."

"Jeez mate you didn't even get your whites dirty. Good on ya mate. Here; have a beer."

"Hey, show me some of those moves. I might need 'em when I get home tonight. The missus is not too happy with me. Here; have a beer."

"Anyone who can belt up Tex and the boys deserves a beer. This one's on me."

"Yer not so bad fer a wog. Good on ya mate. Here; have a beer."

Mick and Owen stood back watching Roberto sink slowly under the weight of bush hospitality. They finally delivered him home to Sally at eleven o'clock that night. They dumped him on the old couch on the verandah. At first, Sally was disgusted and reprimanded the boys for getting Roberto into a drunken state but then she felt some pride when they told her of Roberto's encounter with Tex and his mates.

"Leave him there with the dogs, Sal. He's okay. Bluey and Spot will look after the local hero 'til morning. Give him a steak and eggs for an early breakfast 'cause we're picking him up at seven to go shooting ducks and pigs."

"But we're going back to the city tomorrow," pleaded Sally, anxious about what might happen out in the scrub to her Roberto.

The next morning, they arrived with Owen carrying some work gear from his little brother for Roberto. "Can't take him out in that wog gear, he'd frighten every duck and pig for a hundred miles. See you at lunch time, Sal. That'll give you enough time to drive back this afternoon."

Sally was not very happy when they didn't get back until three o'clock.

"Here you are, Sal. He's all yours. By the way, he's okay. He's a top bloke and you have our blessing, but you had best drive because he'll sleep from here until you get to the big smoke," said Mick with his arm around the shoulders of a very tired, bleary eyed and dirty Roberto.

As Roberto climbed into the passenger seat, he gave Sally a kiss. "Hello darling, we had a great day but I'm a little tired so could you start the driving?"

"Hey Sal, keep your hands on the steering wheel all the way…no hanky panky. This Latin Lover of yours is no Italian Stallion today. Besides, you couldn't do anything in that stupid car. You couldn't even get into the back seat, let alone do anything when you got there," advised Mick.

Sally slapped both of them across the arms in a sisterly manner and then gave them a big hug. "Thanks for looking after him, but I don't know whether he will ever want to come again."

"Don't worry Sally, he'll be here for the Empire Day long weekend," said Owen as he struggled to hold back a belly laugh. "We're going to take him fishing and shooting and I've asked Tex and the boys to take him to the buckjumping at the showground that weekend after the fireworks."

"See ya Sal," shouted Mick smiling from ear to ear.

The Great Flood

"If it rains any more Claude, I'm gunna move down to me son's place so I can dry out fer a while. Me toenails are rotten, me feet stink. Me missus's complainin' bout the mud in the house. The kids are cranky 'cause they can't get out to play. The dogs are gettin' sores, the chooks are orf their layin', the lemon tree's dying with the wet, the fungus is growin' up the wall and the grocery man from the General Store won't come 'cause he can't push his bike through the mud. Wadda yer reckon 'eh?" asked Mike Doyle.

"Yeah mate, like I've said fer the last few weeks, this'll be the big 'un. But it ain't just the rain here at Gubba that's the problem. It's what's happenin' upstream and it's fairly pissin' down at Bomgarra and further up fer a cuppla hundred miles where the river starts," replied Claude Scully.

Andy Watson added his observations while scraping the mud built up on his boots. "Ole Harry wus lucky ta git to his son's weddin' ya know. The young bloke married that sheila from Bomgarra and he had ta drive the family in the ole Austin through the mud all the way. I heard they pushed it most of the way 'cause it kept getting bogged. Took 'em six hours ta get there. Mightin' git back fer a few weeks. I don't think his missus liked the idea of pushin' while Harry drove. Can't see why she'd get excited about that. It's only a bit of mud."

"The trouble is, the big trucks comin' through are churnin' up the crown of the road with deep furrows so that cars bottom on the middle," added Rusty Steele. "Ya can't travel in the table drain 'cause ya'll go down ta yer axle quick as look at ya. Then they drop so much mud in the main street that ya can't even see the one piddling bit of bitumen we've got in town."

Timber Woods sat on an upturned bucket on the levee bank dispirited with the sight of mud and the height of the water in the creek. "That black mud's so sticky it builds up on yer boots so's it's hard ta walk. Squeaky Atkins down at the Railway pub is the only one who's happy. It's the first time he's been able to get his head and shoulders over the top of the bar without standing on his little box."

Rabbit Peters chipped in with his assessment. "We've just had seven years of drought and now we git a record flood. Next thing we'll have all the weeds comin' up an' then the mice and rabbits will eat us out of 'ouse and 'ome. The roos'll cut up the top paddock, the galahs'll eat all next year's crop seeds, the sheep'll git the blowfly rot and dags, the dogs'll git the mange, the kids won't git ta school, the missus is getting' shirty 'cause her vegie garden's buggered, the soles of me boots just rotted out and I can't git inta town ta git me beer. Shit, what else can go wrong? We'll all be ruin'd, that's what."

Things must be bad for Rabbit to string that many words together.

"O D Cologne's getting' into a bit of a stink because he can't get his sano wagon up some of the back lanes to collect the cans. It's not his fault, he's doing the best he can and he makes sure he's looking after the old folk and the widows. They should get off his back," said Dorothy Phillips who had just arrived with a basket of scones and biscuits for the workers on the flood levees.

Timber scratched his face leaving a muddy smear. "This one looks like being the biggest flood on record. Half the town'll go under. The trouble's not so much what comes down the river but what backs up Gubba Creek through the middle of town. The creek hardly ever has any water in it, but now it's two hundred yards wide with dirty water. They say the main bridge over the creek'll go under in three days and we'll have to lift the levee banks to save the low-lying parts of town. It's already starting to back up at the pound and at the bottom of Lee's and Tony Morelli's farms. It won't be long before the cemetery goes under. They reckon a few of the graves will probably go under by tomorrow."

"Don't worry too much about that," laughed Jimmy for light relief. "Old Yappy Morris' grave is at the low end of the cemetery, but he'll be orright 'cause he could talk under water for days without takin' a breath,"

Maud Anderson, who had joined Dorothy, added her touch. "Stinky's grandfather's plot is also down on the low side, but this might be the first time he's ever had a good bath 'cause he certainly didn't have one while he wus alive."

Bluey Morrison couldn't help to put in his penny's worth. "And ya better not do any fishin' downstream of the cemetery after the flood for a few weeks because when ole Mary's grave gets wet her poison tongue'll kill everything down as far as the river. Then there's Pee Wee Pete, who passed on last year. He'll lift the level of the creek at least two inches 'cause he couldn't walk a hundred yards without peeing up against the fence."

"They tell me that you can hear someone hammering down at the cemetery each night," said Speedy Gonzales. "Jack reckons it's old Noah Jacobs comin' up each night to build his big ark because he reckons it'll last for at least 40 days and 40 nights."

Everyone in town had an opinion and they expressed it every day, to anyone within earshot. Everyone was an expert. There was much discussion as to who might be the best at predicting the rises and falls in the levels and there were daily bets on the outcome. The flood, and how everyone was coping, was the only topic of conversation.

The old folk could remember every rise in the river and creek and could retell all the stories of what happened to whom and when. The main beneficiaries of all this talk were the three hotels in town where everyone gathered to get the latest information and predictions on river heights and to attend meetings of the people who coordinated the flood control work.

Big Jim Morris, the local Sergeant of Police, took control, organising all capable men in the district into groups under the lead of key people whom he trusted. Claude Scully and Jock Armstrong controlled the farmers on the north and western sides. Mick Doyle and Andy Watson looked after those in the east and south. Rusty Steele and Timber Woods organised the building of the levee banks on the north side of the creek in town and drew up a twenty-four-hour roster to man the pumps. Rabbit Peters, Bluey Morrison and Jimmy Jackson did the same for the south side.

Big Jim asked Dorothy Phillips from the CWA, Maud Anderson from the Red Cross, Mary Jones from the Show Society and his own wife, Margaret, to coordinate food and drinks for all the workers on the levee banks. Anthony Withers, the Main Roads engineer, and Speedy Gonzales from the Council, kept the trucks and heavy machinery moving up to the areas of greatest need.

The local schools, church halls, School of Arts and the Show Ground pavilions were all cleared to make way for furniture from the houses that had to be evacuated as the water rose. People rescued from flooded homes were taken in by someone nearby who made provision for a few extra mouths to feed and a place for them to sleep. Nobody would go without. Gubba Creek looks after its own.

The upside about floods on the plains is that it takes a long time to reach its peak because the water has to come a few hundred miles from the mountains upstream. The downside is the length of time it stays up and the time it takes to dry out. This is a slow tedious process and tempers get explosive with night after night of manning the pumps and the continual mending of levee banks to protect the houses. To relieve the tension at night, those on roster told stories about recent happenings and they bet on the predicted heights for the next week.

Particularly amusing was the story of Big Mary going to the dunny. A woman of massive proportions, she usually dropped her pants outside before backing in, which prevented her from seeing the large red bellied black snake that had escaped the waters and was coiled around the can. Well, it was a toss-up whether Mary or the red bellied black got the biggest fright and the exit of both from the dunny was a sight to behold. Rumour has it that Mary refused to go to the toilet for three days.

Clarrie Morrison helped ease the tension one night when his wife Flo came at midnight with some hot giblet soup to keep him warm. Clarrie's love life had been somewhat restricted by the fact that he had manned the levee banks every night for three weeks. When he saw that the others had gone to check the pumps around the corner, he grabbed Flo in a bear hug and demanded a cuddle. Flo lost her footing and toppled into the creek pulling Clarrie in with her. They rose like two half-drowned, mud encrusted toads to the cheers from those returning to the main bank.

"Looks like Johnny Weissmuller and Esther Williams are putting on a show for the folks here at Gubba Creek?" chortled Sam Walker.

In the betting stakes, Rusty Steele won most of the money because, all along the river he had mates who fed him accurate information about river heights and he could predict to within half an inch how high the water would be at Gubba a week to ten days ahead.

However, this became a bone of contention between Rusty and Anthony Withers, the Main Roads engineer and Speedy Gonzales from the Council. At their regular meetings with Big Jim, Rusty put up a good case to have more machinery on the north side to increase the height of the levee banks because, if they didn't, most of the houses between the creek and the highway would go under. The engineer would never believe Rusty's predictions because they differed from the official figures he had from head office and he claimed he could no longer get the machinery across the bridge.

As the water rose towards the predicted peak it became obvious to Rusty and his team that the water would break the levee banks and all the houses on the north side of Gubba Creek would go under. He could also see that the main problem on that side of town was the Western Highway. It was built much higher than the surrounding area and prevented the water on the town side from flowing north across the unused common area and away from the town.

Rusty decided to try again to convince the road engineer and council men that he needed action. He paddled his canoe across the swollen creek to the Commercial hotel. As he walked into the main bar, he saw Anthony having a drink in the back room and shouted to get his attention.

"Hey Anthony, if we don't do something within two days on the north side, we'll all go under," he called, showing his increasing frustration. "Now what I want you to do is get a whacking great dozer and rip some channels through the bloody highway in two or three places on the northern side of Sullivan Street. That'll let the water flow through to the common area and take the pressure off our levee banks. How about it, mate? Come on, give us a fair go on the north side."

"You're a dickhead, Rusty," replied Anthony. "I don't know why I waste my time with you. You're always ranting and raving about the north side. Don't you think we've got problems here on this side?"

"I can tell you," shouted Rusty; getting angrier by the minute, "that we have accurate information that the banks on our side will go under in two days and you, you bastard, won't even lift a finger to help us."

"You wouldn't know your bum from your face, Rusty. I have the official figures and I'm telling you that the water won't break the banks on your side. And let me tell you something else," he paused to emphasise the point, "nobody but nobody touches my highway. Do you understand that, or have I got to spell it out in single syllables so you dumb buggers on the other side can comprehend it."

"My predictions have been spot-on every day for the last four weeks," said Rusty "which is more than your official figures. How would your head office know what the levels will be when they are hundreds of miles away in the big smoke. The only water they see is in their whisky?"

"Piss off Rusty and go and do something useful. I've got my work cut out on this side and haven't got time to waste on you whinging dickheads."

Rusty reached through the serving door, grabbed Anthony by the shirt front and hit him square on the nose with a straight right. It took at least ten minutes for the other patrons to separate them. When it was over; Rusty paddled back to the north side to inform the others of the official decision and start working on a plan to evacuate the lowest areas.

Smasher Daley walked slowly over to Rusty. He had stood by Rusty every night throughout the flood crisis. He put his arms around Rusty's shoulder and quietly led him to the box near the pumps. Smasher had recently returned from the war where he had served with distinction working with munitions, defusing bombs and blowing up supply dumps behind enemy lines. He knew no fear and he was not a person to be messed with. He was a great mate to have on your side when the going got tough.

"Hey Rusty me mate," said Smasher, "sit yourself down. Give me a look at that muddy roster in your pocket…there we are, you and I are both on tonight."

"Sure thing, Smasher," replied Rusty, checking his body for the bruises and cuts sustained at the pub. "We're on until two o'clock in the morning. But while we are on duty could you help me work out a plan of evacuation?"

"Better than that, Sunshine. We're gunna drive over to the highway tonight after we hand over to the other blokes at two o'clock. Forget about those bastards on the other side. We won't let the north side go under. Leave it with me mate. I'll organise the gear. I just want you to help me once we're there. See ya tonight old mate. Don't you sweat about it anymore."

That night he and Rusty worked the pumps on the levees until two in the morning. When they finished their shift, they drove off in Smasher's old blitz wagon out to the highway. Nobody saw them go and everyone assumed they had gone home to get some well-earned rest.

****

About ten o'clock the next morning, Big Jim Morris rowed across the creek to the north side, tied his boat to the willow tree, had a chat to the team on the levee banks, and then wandered over to Rusty's place.

"Sorry to wake you up, mate. I know how hard you've been working every night," said Big Jim, "but I'm here to give you some very good news. The level in the creek dropped half an inch overnight. But I have to tell you that your calculations were wrong, and Anthony's were spot on. Then of course, he had access to all that official info from head office. It just goes to show the value of good coordinated information from across the region."

"You don't really expect me to go over there and kiss his arse and give that bastard a big hug, do you Sarge? He's been a thorn in our side all along," said Rusty, wiping the sleep from his eyes.

"No mate. I certainly wouldn't ask you to do that, not until you've had a wash, a shave and put on your make-up. But," Jim paused to make certain that he had Rusty's attention, "there's something that has me puzzled...did you happen to hear two whopping explosions in the early hours of this morning?"

"No Sarge, didn't hear a thing. But that's not surprisin'," replied Rusty, eyes now fully open, arms and shoulders stretching back slowly over the chair, giving him time to think. "When you've been on the banks every night for the last four weeks, nothin' gets through once your head hits the sack. I wouldn't know if a volcano blew up next to the Great Northern. Why do you ask?"

Big Jim got up from the table, walked to the bench and poured himself a glass of water. He drank slowly before continuing. He looked Rusty straight in the eye. "Well, ole son. It seems strange to me that you and Smasher Daley were the only two people in the town who didn't hear those explosions."

"Is that so, Sarge?" Rusty's face was as expressionless as a sack of wheat, except for his eyes that were searching for any movement out the window as a focus of distraction.

"Yes, it is Rusty. Amazing, isn't it? Another thing was amazing last night. The water current was so strong that it broke through the highway in two places and the water is flowing across the common area."

"Must have been a miracle, eh Sarge?"

"Now, before I go back to the town, let me give you a strong bit of advice. You and Smasher confine your drinking to the Great Northern on this side of the creek until the countryside dries out. I don't want to see you at the Commercial for some time. Do you get my point?"

"Clear as crystal, Sarge. I wouldn't want to be mixing with those hoi polloi professional people like engineers that drink over there on the south side, now would I, eh? Thanks for the good news and the advice, Sarge. See ya."

Big Jim rowed his boat back to the other side with a broad smile on his face.

Me Bloody Ute

Taffy Edwards shuffled slowly on his way from his house in Mulga Street to the Railway Hotel to lay a bet with Holy Moses, the local SP bookie, when he heard a deep throated muffler roar down the Great Northern Road, cross the railway line and screech to a halt in a swirl of dust beside him.

Some bloody clown from out of the district, thought Taffy, with a backward glance to see who was in the driver's seat. Taffy paused at the verandah post on the corner of Railway Parade to survey the intruder and the mean machine covered in dirt and locusts. He was trying to see what was the make of the vehicle when the scruff of a driver crawled out, slammed the door, stretched, burped, farted, scratched his groin and called out.

"I bet you ain't seen a bonzer machine like this before, have ya mate?" said the driver swaggering over to say hello to Taffy.

"Yeah, it's me bloody ute, mate. Do ya like it? Pretty good eh, what ya think? Yeah, she's an old cut down model of a '48 Pontiac. Yeah, I've got this great mate up north, more bloody money than sense. He lives up the road on the way to 'Curry. That's Clon- bloody- Curry mate, up the back of Queensland way, best bloody town on God's earth if ya know what I mean. Well, me mate ran this ol' car 'til it couldn't go no further an' left it in the paddock ta rot. So, I gits it fer five quid and I cuts the back orf, then welds a sheet across the back behind the seats. Then I built a tray on the back an' bull bars in the front and some big spotties on a gal' pipe over the roof, an' then put on some bar treads. How da ya like the water buffalo skull on the bar in front eh? Got it out the back of Daly Waters up in the Territory. Scares the shit out uv the roos when they see me comin'. Ya can't see 'em fer dust after I go past, they take orf inta the scrub.

Taffy was anxious to get going to place a bet on the first race but, being a friendly bloke, decided to look interested. "How did you...?"

"How did I fix it, eh?" the driver interrupted. "Well after I got the body fixed, I got underneath and jacked her up, put some extra leaves in the springs, then I put some extra heavy-duty shocks on to toughen her up fer the rough country. I welded a stone guard under the sump, put a gauze guard over the front fer the hoppers. Then I got inta the motor. I bored her out to git some more go and hoot inta the old girl. She was a bit sluggish ta start with...then a heavy-duty battery and plugs, and then Bob's yer uncle, tell your Mum."

Taffy looked in the window across the dash. "How...?"

"How fast can we go, you ask, eh? Well, up where I come from, if ya doing less than a bloody 100 miles an hour, the bloody frill neck lizards will tail-gate ya and then crawl up ya exhaust pipe and stop ya motor stone dead. The ol' girl wus a bit bloody slow

218

before I bored 'er out but now we hoot along pretty bloody quick like, if ya see what I mean."

Taffy walked around to the back. "What…?"

"What's that on the back mate, you ask? Well, I'll tell you. That's me gear. In that box there I got all the stuff I need. It's me swag, me tools, some cookin' gear and some tucker fer me and Bluey…me dog. That's all I bloody need ta git around. If I find a bloody sheila, I shake out the swag ta make sure there's no spiders and I kick Bluey out. Put him under the ute ta give me more room ta do me best."

In two minds whether to move on, Taffy looked back up Great Northern Road. "Where…?"

"Where did I come from; you were gunna ask? Well, me ol' man's got a place about fifty miles out from the Curry. Great cattle country, real men's country and all the bloody women know it. Best place on this man's earth. Why did I leave, I hear ya say? Well, me an' me ol' man had this stand-up blue, we fought 'round the draftin' yard until we couldn't stand no more. He told me to bloody shape up or ship out, so I loaded the ute and pissed orf outa there as quick as an emu with gallopin' diarrhoea. Didn't stop 'til I hit the Territory."

Shuffling towards the pub door, Taffy stopped when the driver continued.

"You want to know what I did up north, mate? I got a job shootin' crocs out from Daly Waters. Great time that, especially when we had ta catch some of 'em live ta take 'em back ta the breedin' farm. We bred 'em fer the skins ya know. Holy shit they can wriggle; bloody well take yer leg orf if yer not careful. Lost me

219

mate up the river one day 'cause he walked inta the river ta git a croc he'd shot, an' another big un took 'im under. Bloody hell, mess everywhere. We couldn't git him out so we buried his hat on the river bank. Great mate he wus, bloody well miss 'im."

Having missed the first race, Taffy was anxious to move on. "Well, I'll be…"

"You want ta know what I did after that? Well, I went to work the cattle on a station near Tennant Creek. I wuz the general rouseabout and stockman. I did everything. It wuz a great place to work, bloody good boss and his missus always looked after us. We'd go out ta shoot camels in the scrub. Met these Swedish sheilas, twins they wus, came to work out there as jillaroos, so I used to take 'em out inta the bush in me bloody ute mate to show 'em a thing or two about this good country, yer know, me being the friendly bloke that I am. And would ya believe it mate; they showed me some parts of the world I never bloody seen before. Shit, they could ride mate? More thrills than ridin' the bloody broncos at the Mount Isa rodeo. Ya wouldn't believe what they could do, an' two of them at the same time workin' on me. They used ta talk about massage or some crap like that. Couldn't understand their lingo much, but who cared. It took me a week ta git over it every time we went out in the scrub.

Taffy pointed to a sticker on the back window. "What…"

"What's the B and S sticker on the back you ask, mate? Well, that's the Bachelor and Spinsters Ball. The last one I went ta wus at Dirran- bloody- Bandi mate. Stone the bloody crows that wus a beaudy…bloody bonzer weekend; rootin', tootin', shootin', scootin' and drinkin' non-stop. Me bloody ute never stopped

220

rockin'. Bluey didn't know what wus goin' on. He wus happy when it wus all over. When we weren't with the sheilas, we wus ridin' in the buckjumps an' camp drafts. Won me a big new belt, best in the flag race, jist missed out on the buck jumpin' prize."

Losing patience, Taffy walked to the doors of the Railway Hotel.

"Would I like a beer, did I hear you ask, mate? Nah. Wouldn't touch that shit. Have ya got a Fourex mate? Only thing I drink. I can't stand the piss ya lot have down here. Wouldn't put it on me Mum's pumpkin patch. And as fer that South Aussie crap, that's nothin' but bloody sheep dip. But then I'm not surprised what all youse Mexicans, south uv the border, drink. Ya also play that funny sheila's footie game with ya little tight shorts. They tell me ya eat chicken and all that kinda shit. Up our way real men eat red meat mate, good steak, hangin' over the sides of the plate, still bellowin'. Our sheilas wouldn't look sideways at youse lot. They want real men. They like it rough and tough and we give 'em what they want. That's why youse bastards pinch all our good footie players 'cause ya need someone ta do the real work in the scrums an' then ta keep all the sheilas happy."

Taffy sat on the front step to rest his legs and his arthritic hip.

"You look like a cane toad restin' in the shade, mate. Yeah, we got plenty of 'em up north as well as snakes and spiders, mate. Yeah mate, but they're no worry. Jist keep an eye open fer them, they's more scared of youse than youse of them. Practice me kickin' with the cane toads. That's why we Queenslanders are the best footie players 'cause we practice with toads and paddy melons. As fer snakes, jist grab 'em be the tail an' give them the ol' whip crack, they don't like that. What about maggots on the meat in the heat, you ask? Yeah, when ya out in the bush fer a few days ya get a few, 'cause ya ain't got no frig. Jist give it a wipe over with the cloth, an' if ya miss a few then its jist a bit extra good tucker fer ya, eh? Ya always git the red back spiders on the dunny seat but if ya don't annoy 'em they won't worry ya. Jist git on an' do what ya got ta do and leave 'em alone. Jist say hello, wipe ya bum an' move on an' leave 'em in peace.

Exasperated, Taffy dropped his head into his hands.

"Did you want ta know if I've ever been to the big city, mate? Yeah, I just come back from there. Bloody shithole of a place. Never agin. Nobody ever smiles or says g'day. Stuck up bunch of shits; sheilas wouldn't talk ta me. I wanted ta take 'em out an' show 'em a good time, like we good guys from up north do, 'cause we look after our sheilas proper-like where I come from. They told me ta git lost. Fair dinkum, I wouldn't give 'em the time uv day. They's not worth a pinch of lizard shit or a pair uv dried up wombat balls. Also, there's cars goin' in all directions, three side-be-side across the road so I jist got up on the footpath and drove through. Then a copper pulled me up and booked me. I wanted ta punch 'is lights out, but me bein' a gentleman, I decided to play it cool, but then the bastard booked me three times on the way out 'cause I wus doin' 90 on the main road. Shit, up our way the snails go faster than that! They said if they ever saw me in town agin they's gunna throw me in the clink. So I jist put me foot down and high tailed it outa there an' left them in me dust. Reckon they're tryin' to work out how me bloody ute can go so fast

222

Taffy rose, stretched and made a second attempt to get in the hotel door.

"Ya wanted ta know what am I gunna do now, mate? Well, I'm gunna go north 'cause while I wus away I heard that me Dad carked it, an' I'm gunna go an' dig up his coffin ta see fer meself that the ol' bastard is really gone. I wouldn't trust them jist tellin' me. I gotta see fer meself. After that I'll jist make sure that me Mum is okay and then I'll head back ta the Territory in me bloody ute with me ol' mate Bluey. I might go back ta the Creek to see if those Swedish sheilas are still there, 'cause ya know, I want ta increase me education like,... 'cause that learnin' is good fer ya, mark my word. A pity youse blokes down south don't git these opportunities like me. And I'll be so far away from those bloody coppers who are still chasing me from the city, they won't find me."

Taffy started to push open the bar door but turned as the stranger shouted.

"Oh shit, there's another copper comin' down the street. Don't like the look of that big bastard, I'm orf outa here, mate. I'll git me bloody ute warmed up and by the time I git to the end of this street ya won't see me fer the dust. After that, I won't stop 'til I cross the border. Then they can all go an' bite their arses fer all I care. They won't find me in the scrub up there. Be seein' ya mate."

Taffy waited until the deep throated roar faded, the dust settled and the bloody ute was out of sight.

"Not if I see you first, mate," he mumbled as he hobbled through the door to get a bet on the third race.